PEARLS ON A BRANCH
Oral Tales

Najla Jraissaty Khoury

Translated from the Arabic by Inea Bushnaq

archipelago books

Originally published as *Hikayat wa Hikayat* by Dar Al Adab,
Lebanon, Beirut, 2014

This edition published by arrangement with Rocking Chair Books and
RAYA, the agency for Arabic literature

Archipelago Books
232 Third Street #A111
Brooklyn, NY 11215

www.archipelagobooks.org

Library of Congress Cataloguing-in-Publication Data Available Upon Request

Cover art: Helen Zughaib

Distributed by Penguin Random House
www.penguinrandomhouse.com

This book was made possible by the New York State Council on the Arts with
the support of Governor Andrew M. Cuomo and the New York State Legislature.
Archipelago Books also gratefully acknowledges the generous support of the
National Endowment for the Arts and
the New York City Department of Cultural Affairs.

PRINTED IN THE UNITED STATES OF AMERICA

PEARLS ON A BRANCH
Oral Tales

for Summer and Yamen

AUTHOR'S NOTE

WHEN I WAS A CHILD, my grandmother told me a story every time I went to visit her. One day she said to me:

"You know, when I was a little girl like you my grandmother used to tell me the stories I am telling you now."

I smiled without saying anything. What a joke! My grandmother a little girl!

Here I am, a grandmother myself, maybe even older than she was at the time. I look back at myself as a little girl and again I smile.

I remember the story of "Eleven." I told my grandmother: I don't understand how someone can name a newborn baby "11."

"It's because those people already had ten children!" she replied. "There is an end to names. There is an end to everything."

The civil war in Lebanon broke out in 1975. It seemed endless. We waited for all of eleven years but still it did not end. It was not until 1990, after 15 years of shelters and darkness that the war finally came to an end.

During that time, I founded a traveling theater company with some friends. We called it *Sandouk el Fergeh*, a kind of Box of Wonders, in recognition of the popular entertainment with the same name, which saw its best hours in the Middle East in the years before the advent of cinema. Our troupe of actors and marionettes produced plays for a good twenty years. Gradually we had to adapt to the war situation and we began to use shadow puppets to perform our stories. That way we were able to put on our shows in marginal areas where electricity was a luxury, in air raid shelters, Palestinian refugee camps, isolated villages, and of course on stage in the towns.

Our plays were largely based on oral tales. I combed the country in search of stories. It was far from easy. Narratives were often muddled, memories failed, rhymes were incomplete. I had to prime the storytellers by prompting childhood memories, reciting the beginning of some rhyme or mentioning titles, like "Eleven." Another problem was that people tend to be suspicious in wartime. I had to be introduced and accompanied by someone known to the tellers. Some women refused to be taped. More than anything I had to be patient.

I often spent hours listening to the narrator – they were mostly women – tell me all about herself, her experiences during the war, her health problems, personal reminiscences, or even some cooking recipe… before I finally ventured to ask: "Who told you stories when you were a child? Which story did you like best?" I had to be on the lookout for stories read in books, seen on television or simply invented. In time I was able to spot these quite quickly. When I eventually found an "authentic" storyteller, I would write out or tape her story, delighted to be listening to it with all the digressions and comments. Almost always I would return to hear the same story again, hoping I would be allowed to tape the teller's voice or at least fill any gaps in my hurriedly written notes.

Whenever a story seemed suitable for a future production, I'd search for alternative versions in different regions and denominations. My goal was to produce a beautiful show. So I'd listen very carefully to every version of the same story. The differences lay more in the details than in the structure of the plot. It was interesting to hear the same story as told on the coast, in the mountains, in urban and rural centers. In border areas with Syria and Palestine, the differences tended to be more superficial.

My friend and translator asked me to include the following incident:

At one point while collecting stories, I happened to be recovering from back surgery and needed to sit upright on a chair. Arriving in one village with my tape recorder, I went to the house where I was expected and found that it consisted of a large room full of women and children. I was given a warm welcome and asked to sit down. But there were no chairs. When they found me a chair, I sat down, feeling confused and embarrassed – everyone else was hunkered down on the floor. The hosts were very sweet, interrupting the narrator time and again to pass around nuts and raisins, almonds, tea and coffee.

That recording turned out to be noisy and incomprehensible. So I had to come back a few weeks later to hear the story told again by the same woman. It was a weekday morning and the children were in school. There were only three or four women present. I had to ask myself whether it was really the same story. When, in the narrative, a jar knocks off the long spout of a water pitcher, the women grinned knowingly; when I asked them why, they laughed outright. I was supposed to catch the sexual reference: a jar (feminine noun) snapping off the spout of the pitcher (masculine). In the earlier session, the storyteller had raced through the sentence, "Bathhouse of the Plants that restores virginity to married women" too fast to be properly understood. Now it was not only clearly pronounced but discussed and commented on.

This made me go about collecting stories in a different way. On the pretext of some failure in my tape recorder or an electric power cut, I would return to ask for a story to be repeated. The second time I went to hear the story I mentioned before, the listeners were all adults with no children present. I paid close attention to the nuances in the choice of words, the comments and body language of the storyteller. It was a revelation: certain stories told by women were for women only.

In these tales, women play the lead roles to the disadvantage of men, especially husbands. Was this revenge for their situation in life? In a society where the men dominate, women use 1001 wiles to assert themselves. At the time when I was collecting the stories, starting in 1978, the average age of the storytellers was sixty. Their instructions were to tell a story exactly as they had heard it as children.

Until the middle of the 20th century, the social structure in the Levant, or Bilad ash-Sham (Lebanon, Syria, and Palestine,) gave precedence to the male. Women, once their housework was done and the children put to bed, were confined (without the benefit of television) to their homes. The men could go out to the coffee house to hear the *Hakawati*, recite the old epics before a strictly male audience. The women visited each other and told stories; stories in which men are dependent on women who are sharper and more intelligent than they are, where women become the true heroines if only through their patience in the face of oppression.

This is the scenario in stories that take place in settings of poverty. By contrast, among kings and rich merchants, men are the powerful "bosses."

Each story is distinctive, but its opening and final lines are often interchangeable rhymed verses. The opening, in particular, might expand over a number of lines or several pages, without a clear connection to the thread of the narrative. The purpose of this *farsheh*, or "mattress," is to catch the listeners' attention and announce that they are heading into an indeterminate elsewhere. "This is what the story will lie upon," says the storyteller.

After twenty years the final curtain was lowered on *Sanduk el Fergeh*. The pursuit of stories, however, continued for memory and for pleasure. These are stories that belong to the human heritage. They are expressions of a distinctive cultural milieu. The notions of good and evil, for example, are not as categorical in them as in Western folktales. Fairies and witches have no equivalent in Arabic; instead there are magicians, male and female, good and bad. An old woman or an ancient man are often ogres, addressed as "Uncle Ogre" or "Mother Ogre." A hero can tame them through his courtesy and deeds.

These stories have an identity all their own. I had no right to keep them hidden in my drawer; I felt it a duty to share them. I chose one hundred stories from among the most popular and published them in Arabic in 2014, exactly as I received them from the mouths of the storytellers, who told them as they had heard them from their parents and grandparents when they were children.

Out of the hundred stories published in Arabic, Inea Bushnaq and I chose thirty for this book. I hope that they will give the reader as much pleasure as they gave me listening to them.

— Najla Jraissaty Khoury

TRANSLATOR'S INTRODUCTION

THE FOLKTALES IN THIS COLLECTION, oral survivors from a pre-literate era, resemble a quilt made with the fabrics of well-loved clothes. Just as patches of cloth in a quilt are arranged in different combinations to form a design, traditional folk motifs appear and reappear in a variety of settings and plots to shape the stories. One prince falls in love with the grocer's daughter next door, another can't take his eyes off the Bedouin girl he sees on his way to the hunt, all to the horror of the royal mothers. Here a golden anklet, and there a voice heard out of an open window, inspire obsessive love for their unknown owners. A songbird with green feathers reveals one crime and a speaking nightingale another. In the stories, love conquers all, but inevitably there are obstacles on the way to the happy ending. These are tales told by women to women so, not surprisingly, the main characters often are young women with remarkable courage, wit, and endurance. Whatever their unfortunate circumstances at the beginning, whether poverty or oppression, they are the heroines in the end.

The thirty texts gathered here have been chosen from one hundred tales, recorded and transcribed by Najla Jraissaty Khoury and published in Beirut in 2014. Captured on tape, these are verbatim renderings of the storytellers speaking. The present translation, like the transcriptions, adheres word for word to the Arabic original. The aim is to allow the English reader to listen in as the storytellers, older women living in Lebanon in the last quarter of the 20th century, pass on the stories they had heard in childhood. Only in the verses that ornament many of the stories does the English sometimes need a few added words to be comprehensible.

"Once upon a time," the opening to English and European tales seems to promise an account of actual happenings. The Arab narrator is not so certain; she begins her story with the phrase *kan ya ma kan*: it was or it was not – it happened or it did not. When magic and supernatural beings take part in human affairs, how can one be sure? *Kan ya ma kan* is generally followed by the rhyming *fi qadim az-zaman*, "in the oldness of time." Often a few more verses with the same rhyme follow, questions to the audience – do they want to listen or do they prefer to go to bed? – as if asking permission to speak. At times, God, the Prophet, the Virgin Mary, or a local saint might be invoked in the introductory verses.

It is still customary among older people in Arabic-speaking countries to pronounce the name of God, *bismillah*, as a blessing, before embarking on any enterprise: starting the car for a journey or preparing to knead bread at home. Over the entrance of houses one often sees, as a blessing or for protection, the words, "It is by the will of God", *ma sha' Allah* i.e. built not by the hand of man alone. In one of the stories, a woman sings praises of her niece's house then automatically repeats, "It is God's will!" This is almost a required expression after praise, when admiring a baby, congratulating a graduate, or celebrating any other success. It invokes divine protection and averts the evil eye of envy. All the more then, would a story-teller feel the need for blessing and protection when embarking on a story involving powerful jinns – beings believed to exist invisibly alongside human beings.

More elaborate than the handful of rhymes following *kan ma kan*, there is a long stretch of fantasy and nonsense rhyme called the *farsheh*. Literally, the *farsheh* is the soft bedding stored in a corner during the day and rolled out onto the floor at night, turning the living space into a bedroom. It is the equivalent of a red carpet rolled out for the stories about to be heard. At a storytelling session, it is the prelude to the main event. In the manner of a traditional evening's entertainment, a sample *farsheh* precedes the rest of the narratives in the book. This particular text was part of a much longer recited verse. A num-ber of the tales have their own, shorter introductory nonsense rhymes. Even without paying full attention to the words, lis-teners settling into their places for the storytelling would enjoy the lilt of the *farsheh*'s rhyme.

In classical Arabic poetry, a single rhyme can be sus-tained for hundreds of verses, delighting and surprising listeners with the skill of the poet in achieving the repeated echo. Such an attempt in English, were it even possible, would be monotonous. Arabic has the advantage of considerable flexibility. Almost all words grow out of three-letter and, to a lesser extent, four-letter roots. The root letters can be extended and tweaked to have very different meanings; a single word can express number, gender, case, and tense all at the same time. This facilitates word play and rhyme, both of which are popular oral arts. There are competitions held for ex-tempore versifying, and even at an informal dinner table, guests might engage in a round of ad lib verse, teasing those present or commenting on the politics of the day. In folktales, simple verses with homespun images, some formulaic, some playful, are inserted to highlight moments of drama.

Folktales everywhere address the same human needs and passions. The differing cultures, however, lend their separate coloring to the way their stories express love and hate, achieve justice, defeat oppression. A distinctive feature of the Arabic-speaking countries was the patriarchal family system. For centuries it served as the individual's main support in the community. In return, personal aspirations had to cede before the demands of family welfare; family honor and property had to be preserved at all costs. To that end marriage between first cousins was the preferred arrangement. In stories, like "The Girl Who Had No Name," where a youth chooses a stranger as his bride, the resentment of his rejected first cousins is the trigger for the unlikely events that propel the plot. Whether they are blood relatives or not, fathers- and mothers-in-law are called 'Paternal Uncle' or 'Aunt' because that is the assumed norm for the relationship. Adults, once they are parents, are identified by the name of their firstborn son rather than by their own names as in *Abu Suleyman* and *Umm Suleyman*, Father-of Suleyman and Mother-of-Suleyman. One of the worst curses in Arabic is to wish childlessness upon a person. Interestingly, childless women in the stories pray for baby girls. Fathers want sons and one father, having no male child, sends his daughter to school as he would a boy; girls in the stories are taught at home. As if family were the sole model for relationships, strangers are called Brother, Sister, Aunt, Granny, depending on the age and gender of the person addressed.

The woman in the patriarchal family is regarded as a protégée of her men folk, her father and her brothers. Certainly the stories demonstrate loyalty and protectiveness among siblings: brothers ready to face ogres and hazardous travels for the sake of a sister and sisters refusing marriage in order to devote themselves to prayer for a sick brother's recovery. To this day, fathers, protectors of the family, keep a sharp eye on their daughters, especially as any hint of misbehavior by an unmarried young woman can stain her family's honor. In the stories, the father, fond and indulgent as he may be towards his daughter, becomes suddenly harsh when he suspects her of unseemliness. A recurring theme is the bold young woman who resists her father's will and takes matters into her own hands. She rides away dressed in men's clothes, or pretends to be a humble serving girl and devises any number of ingenious tricks to achieve her goal and eventually marry the man of her choice. Beyond the success of her plans, the girl's ultimate vindication is to see her father's tears and remorse when the family is finally reunited. To be sure, the sons in the stories also create problems. However, when they fall in love with the wrong girl, they are not forced into lengthy struggles or harrowing adventures; their mothers quickly relent and go themselves to ask for the girl's hand on behalf of their sons.

While rebellious daughters venture bravely into the world, there are quieter girls who realize their hopes through patience and endurance. This too takes courage. In a number of stories the girls are subjected to what amounts to a trial by silence. A young bride is advised not to speak until her husband utters a certain phrase. She maintains her silence even under threat of divorce and after the husband acquires a second wife, a co-wife. (Islam permits a man to marry up to four wives with the proviso that he maintain and love them equally.) Accepting hardship and heartbreak without complaint, these girls also succeed at the last. One device for unraveling their mounting woes is a "stone of patience." Chipping away at it with a knife, a girl unburdens herself by listing her sorrows in sing-song.

Talking aloud to the stone, a form of folk therapy perhaps, also allows the girl to be overheard by her husband or her oppressor. And so the truth is learned, innocence is proven and all ends well.

As they thread their way through the challenge of family relations – including the usual jealous sisters, overbearing husbands and wicked stepmothers – the young men and women of the stories are lured or stray into realms of magic and the supernatural. Here are palaces with rooms through which run rivers of silver and gold and gardens with flowers that talk in rhymes. Peacocks lay eggs that make girls pregnant; combs can turn into dense forests in an emergency and mirrors into lakes.

Inhabiting this parallel world are the Jinn, and they take many spirit forms. Hairy ghouls with sharp fangs and a taste for human flesh are the monsters most frequently met with. Unlike the ogres of other cultures, they can be good as well as evil. A few respectful words or some personal service, barbering or bathing, will win a ghoul over. No longer a threat, he becomes a kindly father figure and a source of helpful information. A female ghoul will be mollified by some volunteer house cleaning. There are Jinn in the shape of bearded old men, some benign and some malicious. One demon demands the right to suck at will the blood from a young girl's finger; another dresses the tips of a woman's fingers with gold after every encounter. One spirit adopts a runaway girl and raises her to be fit to marry the king's son; another hounds the girl who disobeys him and transforms her into a mangy dog.

A story about spirits gives free rein to the imagination to recount what in real life is impossible and invisible. A story also gives the woman storyteller the freedom to speak of what in real life would be unacceptable. Adultery and illegitimate birth, cultural taboos, seem to be treated fairly casually. Sexual innuendo, sometimes quite broad, is permitted for amusement, especially when the joke is on the men.

Underlying each plot there usually hides some didactic message. No need to spell out a moral at the end of the story. As elsewhere, compassion is rewarded and evil always punished. A cardinal virtue in Arab culture is hospitality: the penniless goatherd, who slaughters his only animal to feed a guest, later happens upon a chest filled with gold. Acceptance of fate is wisdom. "What is written on the brow will be seen by the eye," goes one saying. Contentment is touted and plain folk living in tents are shown to be happier than princes.

Even the handful of children's tales in this collection reflects the customs of the culture and the tenor of the stories. The little mouse that wants to be married gets her mother's consent only when her suitor is another mouse and a first cousin. Like women in the stories, the little mouse is boss; she makes every decision for her husband. This is true of the frog's wife also: she calls the shots from the moment she leaves in a huff to take refuge in her paternal home, until she deigns to rejoin her distraught husband at the very end.

In addition to the adventures of the characters in the folktales, ranging from royal princes to orphan girls spinning wool for their living, the modern reader may appreciate the unexpected glimpses into a simpler way of life that is rapidly becoming "once upon a time and long ago." The jealous sisters in one story conspire on the flat roof of their house where they are stationed to keep away the birds from the family's wheat, spread out to dry in the sun. A fond village bridegroom, proud of his wife, places nails where they will catch her veil so everyone attending the wedding feast may see the beauty of her uncovered face.

Growing out of almost every flat rooftop nowadays are television aerials thick as a crop of barley and satellite dishes fat as prize melons. The gentle pleasure of hearing a story from a parent or grandparent is being eclipsed by the light shining from the television. Najla Jraissaty Khoury's painstaking rescue mission to preserve the oral tradition gives the age-old tales another life, in print, that will prevent them from being forgotten altogether.

THE FARSHEH

An old woman,
Who looks like a hag
With grey hairs that sag
And a comb in her bag,
Walks with a limp and a hop
Till she comes to a grocer's shop.
"Young man, what is your name?
You set my soul aflame."
Says the young man:
"They call me Taktakan."
"Do you sell cream and do you sell wine?" she asks.
"And perfume in crystal flasks?
It is for a girl, radiant as the sun at noon,
A full-bodied young woman with a beautiful face,
She can say to the mid-month moon,
'Set! Let me shine in your place.'
Her hair? Ropes fit to tether camels!
Her cheeks? Two Damascene apples!
Her lips? Neat and thin,
A coffee cup's rim!

Her forehead? The morning star!

Her nostril? A curved scimitar!

Her eyes? Eyes of a gazelle grazing on the hill!

Her brows? Lines drawn with a fine-cut quill!

She is sweeter than Turkish delight

All of Istanbul has no fairer sight."

The young man felt faint and said with a cry:

"Stop, Old Woman, stop or I'll die!

Tell me what I must do,

I'll give my life and treasure too

If only I could find her!"

She said:

"You'll need a turban, Indian cashmere, for your head,

For your back, a shawl of woven mohair thread.

Ride a pedigree horse with a lively trot

Fill your purse with all the gold you've got.

You'll come to where three mansions stand

The finest in the land

One richly furnished

One lately varnished

One notched with gold untarnished.

Pull the bell

Hear the knell

A young girl will bid you welcome…

The young man wept:

"Enough! Old Woman, say no more!

My head is lost, my heart is sore!"

H E WENT TO HIS STOREHOUSE and put up for sale all the goods he owned. When the store was empty, with nothing left to sell, his purse was filled with one thousand, one hundred dinars of gold. So the young man went to the cloth merchant:

"O Hajj, do you sell cashmere?" he asked.

"Yes," said the merchant, unrolling the cloth along his arm. One arm's length then another, the merchant began to measure and the youth to wind until they had a turban fit for a sheikh.

Next the youth went to visit a man who owned a horse.

"O Hajj, will you lend me your horse for an hour or so?" he asked.

"Anything you want, dear fellow, take it and welcome!" said the man. This was the pedigree horse. The young man jumped into saddle, put the turban on his head, and went to his friend old Hajj Hassan.

"O Hajj," he said, "Will you let me borrow your shawl for an hour or so?"

"Gladly," said Hajj Hassan, "Take it."

It was a mohair shawl that people wore in bygone days and used as a cloak. The young man threw it round his shoulders and rode to the place the old woman described.

He arrived where three mansions stood,
The finest of the neighborhood:
One richly furnished,
One lately varnished,
One notched with gold untarnished.
He pulled the bell
He heard the knell
A young woman with a tray,
Came out to say
"Welcome to you, Taktakan!"

She offered him coffee and he drank it. When he put back the cup, she said:

"Now lay your purse, one thousand, one hundred dinars of gold, on the tray and stay. Sit here and wait, we'll not be late."

"Your wish, my command," said the youth.

She took the gold and he sat down. One hour, two hours passed. Waiting is hard and he was bored. He looked out the window. There, as far as the eye could see, was a garden and in it grew all that lip or tongue might crave: every kind of fruit and plant.

"I need some air," he thought. "I'll take a turn outside."

As he paced the garden he saw a henna shrub, tall and luxuriant – exalted be the Creator! From here to there, its scent hung heavy on the air. The young man found it pleasing.

"By God, I'll pick me a flower and sniff it as I go," he said. He reached up to snatch the bloom but the plant rebuked him:

"Hands off, or I will call a curse on you!

My mistress mocks: she neither loves nor likes you."

"O God's wonder, you can talk?" he asked.

"I am Henna," said the plant,

"I can speak and also sing,

I'm a guest at all weddings.

My deep red henna dye

Adorns each and every bride."

The young man left and continued walking. On his path there was an apple tree its branches bending, weighed down with fruit. From each stem hung two apples – one red, one green – praised be the Creator!

"I think I'll pick me an apple," said the youth. But as he stretched his hand towards the tree it said:

"Hands off, or I will call a curse on you!

My mistress mocks: she neither loves nor likes you."

"O God's wonder, you can talk?" asked the young man.

The tree said:

"Of course I have the gift of speech!

I am the one whose fruit tastes best,
I keep my apples out of reach
For he who picks one knows no rest."

The young man left. Around him grew fruits and flowers of every kind that he dared not touch. Then he glimpsed a shimmer far ahead. He ran to see and found a pavilion – a glittering wonder to behold! Four gold pillars were the base; the walls inlaid with pearls and gems; diamonds and rubies, faceted in varying ways. He saw a young woman walking towards him with roses preceding her and jasmine following as she came. Beautiful she was as the old woman had said. One look and the young man fell apart! Every bone in his spine was loosened and all his strength deserted him. He sank to the ground unable to move either arm or leg.

"Get up!" the young woman said, giving him a push with her foot. "He who seeks women that are fair, must not groan and cry despair. Get yourself up!"

She pushed and pulled and made the young man sit upright. "O Taktakan," she said, "Will you let me rest on your knee a while?"

She placed her head upon his lap and closed those gazelle eyes. In her sleep, now she blushed and then was pale. O Lord, the tints in her face! Roses and lilies! They maddened the young man till he began to sob. One hot tear fell on the young woman's cheek. She awoke and said:

"What is this, O Taktakan, burning coal or a tear of woe?"

"A tear, dear Lady," said the youth.

"What makes you cry?" she asked.

"I lament love unrequited," he said.

"Love unrequited?" She screamed. "What did you hope for, Cur? What more, Son of a Cur?"

She slapped him once on this side of his head and once on that. Suddenly, without knowing how it happened, there he was, back in his grocer's store, buying and selling as before!

AHAA

*There was this Bedouin. He met a young woman. He was
thirsty. She was carrying a sheepskin full of milk.*

He said, "Will you let me have a sip?"

"Be my guest," she said and offered him the leather sack.

When he was done, she said:

"If I knew your name I would wish you good health!"

"My name is hidden in your face," he said.

*"It must be Hassan, as in beautiful?" she asked. "Good
health to you, O Hassan!"*

*"Had I known your name," he said, "I would have said,
'Thank you!'"*

"You can find my name in your amulet."

*"My amulet contains a charm so you must be Fitna,"
he cried, "Your beauty, O charming Fitna, holds Hassan
captive!"*

T HERE WAS OR THERE WAS NOT, in a former time, in an
age long past, an Emir, a prince of the Arab tribes.

Every year he would travel through the villages of his
territory to collect taxes and rent. One day, while he was on his
rounds, he felt thirsty, very thirsty. So he headed to the nearest

spring. From a distance he could see someone standing by the water, a figure slender as a poplar: a tree with a trunk straight as a column, topped by a full crown of leaves. It was a young woman filling her water jar. Her waist was like the waist of a gazelle. He went up to her and said:

"Will you let me drink from the mouth of your jar?"

She lifted the jar onto her shoulder and leaned towards him. He went up close and drank.

"Honey!" he said.

The girl smiled. He asked her what she was called and who was her father.

"Aaha," was all she said.

He thought she was sighing. He promised himself that he would find her the following year. He would be ready then to ask for her hand in marriage.

One day goes and another comes. Day in, day out, the prince kept thinking about the girl by the water. When a year had passed he mounted his horse and rode back to that same village. He could see that the place was preparing for a wedding: there was finery and music and a feast spread out. When he reached the village spring he found an old woman getting water. So he asked her about the celebration.

"Today is the wedding of the most beautiful of all the girls in the village," she said. "She is marrying her uncle's son, her first cousin. You are welcome, if you would like to come."

He asked the name of the bride.

"Aaha," she said.

He realized that Aaha was her name and this was her wedding day. So how could he ask for her hand in marriage? He sat by the side of the spring with his head in his hands. The old woman could see that he was distressed. She asked him what the matter was.

"Can you keep a secret, Granny?" he asked. "Can you hold a confidence?"

"Like a bottomless well," she said.

So he told her what had happened the year before: how he had felt a great love for Aaha and that, night and day, he could think only of her.

"How can I help you?" she asked, "Today is her wedding, they are celebrating even now."

He asked the old woman to empty the water out of her jar – which she did. Then he filled it with honey. The old woman placed the jar on her shoulder and joined the revelers. People ran to help her with the heavy load but she refused. She circled round the wedding party three times, then she stopped in front of Aaha. Everyone present looked on, curious about her strange behavior.

The old woman tilted the jar so that Aaha could have a taste of the honey. Then she spoke in a voice loud enough for all to hear:

"Aaha,

Take a taste from the mouth of this jar.
Take a look, he who filled it is not far.
If a man lost something dear
Can he find it after a year?"
"Need you ask?" Aaha replied,
"If the thing he lost is truly dear
Yes, he will find it after a year!"

Now the bridegroom, who was her cousin, her uncle's son, was standing close by. He saw the look in Aaha's eyes. He saw how she was transformed once she tasted the honey and heard the old woman's words. So he said to his uncle, Aaha's father:

"O my Uncle,
Listen to your daughter.
Understand what she means!
I cannot be groom or suitor
Where a heart to another leans!"

So, in the midst of the wedding, the bridegroom gave up his right to his first cousin so that she might live and be happy with the one she preferred.

She had chosen the Emir of the Arabs and the Emir of the Arabs had chosen her.

The wedding guests dispersed to hill and dale
And I traveled here to tell you the tale.

ABU ALI THE FOX

There was or maybe there was not,
But listen to this tale that I have got...

THERE WAS A FOX. His name was Abu Ali al-Wawi, Abu Ali the Fox. He loved to eat red meat and chicken too. And, of course, he loved his wife and his two young cubs. But he felt hungry, hungry all the time.

One day, Abu Ali the Fox went out of his den, leaving his wife behind with his son Daybess and his daughter Daybessa. He had decided that he would become a devout ascetic and abstain from eating all flesh whether meat or chicken. He gathered some olive pits that he strung together like prayer beads and hung them from his neck. Then he wrapped a turban round his head. In short, he turned himself into a Dervish.

With shoulders bent and head bowed to the ground, he shuffled along slowly, praising God and mumbling prayers. Only his eyes were quick, glancing right and left, taking note of everything in sight.

Ha! Out of the corner of one eye he saw a hen and heard her calling:

"O Abu Ali the Fox!"

He made no reply and did not turn his head but continued

on his way pretending he did not see or hear. The hen darted after him as fast as she was able and shrilled:

"What's up with you, Abu Ali the Fox? Why don't you look round when I call? Where are you off to?"

The fox stopped. Without turning, he said in a husky whisper:

"I am renouncing the world, dear Sister. I have foresworn the consumption of chicken. From now on my diet will consist of nothing but plants and herbs."

The hen was astounded. She said:

"Are you calling me Sister? Why, you are my worst enemy!"

"We are all brothers and sisters. We are one family." said the fox. "What I wish for now is to live in peace and quiet. I am going on the pilgrimage, on the Hajj, Sister. But don't tell anyone."

The hen said:

"Going on the Hajj? I beg you, take me with you. I won't tell a soul."

He said:

"I'll take you with me on one condition: that you keep your distance. Don't walk too close to me. I don't want anyone who sees us to think I am planning to eat you up."

The hen thanked him and obediently followed, walking a few steps behind him.

The fox continued on his way walking slowly, praising God

and muttering prayers. But his eyes were alert. They surveyed everything around him.

Ha! From the corner of his eye he glimpsed a rooster and heard him calling:

"Hey! Abu Ali the Fox!"

But he pretended he hadn't seen or heard him. So the rooster ran up to him and squawked at the top of his voice:

"Where are you going, Abu Ali? What is the matter with you today? Didn't you see me?"

Abu Ali the Fox stopped. Without looking round he replied, with a voice low and hoarse:

"I have renounced the world. I have made a vow. Never again will I eat roosters. From now on I will eat only fruit and vegetables."

The rooster said:

"But you have been feeding off my fathers and forefathers for as long as anyone can remember."

"The past is past. It's history," replied the fox. "Today I want to make my peace with everyone before I go on the Hajj."

"The Hajj?" cried the rooster, "I beg you, take me with you."

"I'll take you with me," said the fox. "But kindly walk behind me a little way. I don't want those who see us to think that I want you for my dinner."

The rooster thanked him and, doing as he was told, walked along beside the hen.

The fox went on walking, walking slowly, until he met a partridge who asked him:

"Where are you going, Abu Ali the Fox?"

"Haven't you heard?" said the fox. "I have renounced the world and have vowed to eat no birds or fowl anymore. I am on my way to the Hajj with the rooster and the hen. Look, there they are."

"But you are a born swindler, O Abu Ali the Fox. And you are not about to change your ways," said the partridge. "How am I to believe that you have decided to atone for your sins?"

The fox shook his head and softly said:

"I have taken an oath, Sister. I have sworn."

"In that case," said the bird, "please take me on the Hajj with the others."

"Come with us then," said the fox. "But walk at some distance behind me and without talking."

So the partridge walked behind the fox along with the rooster and the hen, all of them humbly muttering prayers as they went. They walked and walked until they were tired and hungry and parched with thirst. The sun had set. Abu Ali the Fox said:

"Night has darkened, O my brothers. Let us rest here before continuing on our way. We can feast on grasses and seeds. By the grace of God, they are abundant at our feet."

The birds pecked here and there and then went to roost.

All were fast asleep except for Abu Ali the Fox's stomach. For a week now he had subsisted on nothing more than bread and olives and all night long his stomach growled and rumbled. He was very, very hungry.

Next morning they all woke up. The birds foraged for their breakfast, picking up a seed here and a blade of grass there. As for Abu Ali the Fox, he sat watching them, thinking about the juicy flesh under their feathers and wondering which one of them to choose for his meal.

"O my brothers," he said. "It is true that I have taken a vow to be vegetarian. However, I am going to make an exception: I will abstain from all meat except for the flesh of sinners. And you, O Hen, have sinned grievously."

"Me?" shrieked the hen. "What have I done wrong?"

"All mothers," said the fox, "call their young to nurse them. But with you, O Hen, it is a lot of cackle and no milk."

"But…" began the hen.

"No ifs, ands, or buts," interrupted the fox and, with that, he pounced on the hen and ate her up.

The travelers resumed their journey. The rooster and the partridge walked ahead in silence and dread while the fox kept an eye on them, following behind. Not many hours went by before the fox's stomach began to rumble again. He was hungry. Eating the hen had given him an appetite. So he was ready to select his dinner.

"O brothers," he said. "Let us rest awhile. It is time for a midday meal." And he sat gazing at the rooster and the partridge as they pecked at the ground for grasses and seeds.

"Yes, dear Brothers," he said, "I have vowed to eat no birds; no birds, that is, unless they are sinners. And you, O Rooster, have sinned greatly."

The rooster stopped looking for seeds and cried, "I a sinner? On the contrary, I crow in the morning for the dawn to bring the light of day."

"Yes, you crow and crow. But day dawns with or without a rooster's crowing!" said the fox. And before the rooster could say another word, he fell upon him and devoured him.

Abu Ali the Fox walked on, with the partridge trotting in front of him silent and afraid, until night fell. Once more Abu Ali the Fox's stomach growled with hunger.

"It is suppertime, O Partridge," said the fox. "And I do declare that your sin is the biggest of all."

"How can I be a sinner?" said the partridge. "I trouble no one. I make no sound. I neither crow nor sing. I am barely able to fly. I have to build my nest on the ground."

The fox responded:

"The proverb says: 'If you can't afford to feast on veal, go hunt a partridge for your meal.'"

"What will you get out of me?" pleaded the partridge. "A dish of boiled wheat is more filling!"

"Good for nothing, are you?" said the fox, "That is reason enough to chew your bones."

Screeching as loudly as she could, the partridge said:

"It's true! You are right! Only give me a moment for a prayer, the time for a couple of genuflections before you gobble me up."

Then the partridge moved to one side and, gathering all her strength, she batted her wings again and again until she lifted herself onto the branch of a tree.

"My only sin, O Abu Ali the Fox," she said, "was that I believed you when you told me you were making amends for your past sins."

So the fox remained hungry without any supper. And the partridge hopped from twig to twig happy in her freedom and her escape.

THE SUN HER MOTHER,
THE MOON HER FATHER

It happened or maybe it didn't.
Let us tell stories that amuse and delight.
Even if we sleep a little later tonight
Some on pillows stitched with pearls and coral rings;
Some on pillows full of lice and crawling things.

ONCE THERE WERE THREE GIRLS. Their mother and father were dead and they lived together in a small house at the outskirts of town. From their parents they had inherited a cow. Every day they milked their cow and fed it grass.

After milking one day, the young women set the milk to cool on a flat rock near the house. This was at sunset. Night fell and the girls forgot about the milk. It remained outside uncovered in the moonlight. Next morning at sunrise the youngest girl saw that the cream lay thick on the surface of the milk. Its silvery whiteness tempted her: it looked like pearls in sunlight. Dipping her finger she took a mouthful. How soft and sweet and fresh it was! She tasted it again and then some more until there was no cream left on the milk.

Well, the girl became pregnant.

Her sisters were thunderstruck and began to scold her.

"O dear Lord!" said the girl. "No one has visited me nor

have I gone to see anyone. No one knows me and I know no one."

Her sisters asked her whether she had left the house at any time without their knowing. She said she had only gone as far as the flat rock in the morning and had eaten the cream off the milk without telling them. But she had never gone any farther.

One of the sisters said, "All night long the face of the milk saw the face of the moon. Then, in the morning, it saw the face of the sun. The moon and the sun! The sun and the moon!"

Now they understood what had happened.

The nine months passed quickly and the young woman gave birth to a girl. Her sisters pulled the infant from her belly. It was a child of luminous beauty. And no wonder, with the sun for her mother and the moon her father! The three sisters cared for her; they taught her what they knew and raised her till she was grown. How they loved her! Nothing that she asked for did they refuse her. The anklets she wore were made of gold.

One day the girl joined her friends for an outing. As they were splashing barefoot in a lake nearby, one of the girl's anklets fell into the water. She looked and looked but could not find it. So she went home without it.

Some days later, the king's son happened to be riding past the lake. His horse was thirsty. Every time it bent its head down to the water to drink, it would flinch and step back. The prince slid off the saddle and went to see what the matter was. What he saw was sunlight bouncing off a golden anklet that glistened in the clear water. He reached down and pulled it out. Very carefully he examined it, turning it over in his hands. "Beautiful! And how delicate," he said to himself and he took it with him back to the palace.

To his mother he said:

"Mother, O Mother, lay cobwebs on my bed
I burn with fever, I'll soon be dead."

She said:

"God save your heart and keep your soul! Tell me, what is wrong?"

He opened his hand and gave her the anklet:

"I want to marry the owner of this anklet or else I'll die of longing."

His mother told him that she would find him the girl and that she would begin the search the very next morning. Then he said:

"I beg you, dear Mother, when you find her say: 'I want you as my daughter-in-law.' Do this, even if she turns out to be a slave girl."

Next morning, the king's wife asked her friend, an old woman who lived in the palace, to undertake the errand and bring back any news.

The old woman took out a platter of gold, placed the anklet on it and covered it with a silken kerchief. Carrying this with her, she went from house to house, from building to building, knocking on doors and asking questions. She toured the city from end to end but found no trace of the girl. When she returned she said to the king's wife:

"I circled the entire city. I could not find her."

The king's wife said:

"Tomorrow go out to the edge of town. She may live in one of the modest houses there."

So the old woman returned to her task and knocked on doors and asked questions until she came to the house of the three sisters. When the young girl opened the door and saw her anklet she cried out, "That is my anklet, O Aunt!"

"So where is the one that matches it?" asked the old woman.

The girl lifted the hem of her robe and the old woman noticed how neat and white her bare ankle was. She compared the two golden jewels and when she was certain that they were a pair she hastened back to the palace. She informed the king's wife that the girl was young and beautiful, like the full moon on its fourteenth night.

The king's wife brought the good news to her son. Then she went and asked for the girl in marriage.

Now the preparations began. They brought her gold jewelry and new clothes and everything a bride might need. They adorned her and dressed her in wedding finery. The sheikh was summoned, and the marriage contract signed. Then the music sounded and celebrations continued for seven days and seven nights.

Before the girl left with her husband, her mother said to her:

"Go my child. God be with you! They say, 'If you talk to a wall it will answer if only with an echo.' May God answer my prayer and grant you joy."

Her aunts instructed her:

"Because he is the king's son you have to maintain your own position. Don't say one word to him until he mentions your mother the sun and your father the moon."

When the king's son saw the girl face-to-face he forgot the dancing, the wedding, and the song. Her beauty held him like a spell. He took her by the hand and led her to his chamber. He asked:

"Tell me, shall we eat or play or sleep?"

She did not respond.

"Speak to me! Are you mute?" he asked.

She remained silent.

So it went, on the first day and the second day and the third.

"Love of my heart! Light of my eyes!" he pleaded. But it was no good. He was at a loss what to do. One day he asked the chambermaid:

"Does she talk to you?"

"She talks not only to me, but to the furniture, the wardrobe and the chair. Everything obeys her!" she said.

The king's son was annoyed. He told the girl that he would discard her if she did not answer him. She kept silent. Then, after a while, he threatened to divorce her. Still she did not speak. Finally he told her that he was going to take a second wife, to be her co-wife. She said nothing.

The king's son lost all patience. He married his cousin, his uncle's daughter, warning her to have nothing to do with his first wife. They lived in a palace facing his old home. The new wife would steal glances at the old palace hoping to catch a glimpse of the first wife or hear something about her.

One day the king's son said to the maidservant:

"Go to my old wife and tell her that your master feels like eating fish today."

The maidservant went and gave the message:

"My master sent me to say that he feels like eating fish today."

"You and your master are both welcome!" the first wife said.

Then, seated in her place, she pointed to the cooking stove and said, "Come!" The stove moved of its own accord, step-by-step, till it was at her side. Then she pointed at the frying pan: "Come!" The frying pan slid off the shelf and came. "Olive oil, pour! Fire, catch light!" Just so: pointing her finger and giving her orders without moving from her seat!

The maid could not believe her eyes; she sat open-mouthed, nailed to her spot.

When the oil was good and hot the first wife lowered her fingers into it. Stretching her fingers to show the span of her hand, she said: "The hand, my hand: the fish, my fish!" Ten times she spread her palms while the oil dripped from her fingers. Then she took ten fried fishes out of the pan, wrapped them in paper and gave them to the maidservant saying:

"I wish you and your master good health!"

The maidservant received the fish and hurried back to her master. She reproached him for marrying again when his first wife was so beautiful, and then described everything she had seen. The second wife heard it all and as soon as her husband left, she called the maid:

"Why are you so taken with her? Come and see for yourself! Anything she does I can do too – and do it better! Is she better than I am? No, I am as much the prince's wife as she is!"

Sitting cross-legged on the floor she pointed to her cooking stove and said:

"Come, stove!"

The stove did not move. She raised her voice and repeated, "Come!" Then she shouted a third time. But the stove did not stir nor did the frying pan slide off the shelf or the fire light itself. So the second wife got up, put the frying pan on the stove and lit the fire to heat the oil. She dipped her fingers into the bubbling pan but before she could finish saying, "This hand, my hand…" there was a sizzling sound and she snatched out her hands. Her fingers were fried to a crisp and her scream, piercing as a whistle, could be heard right through the kitchen walls.

The maid ran to her lady's husband wailing and weeping:

"God keep you whole, Master. My mistress is on fire! She is nothing but a heap of cinders."

Another time the second wife noticed her rival sitting at the window weaving a sash of rose-colored wool. The first wife invited her to visit. But she said:

"My husband has forbidden me to talk to you."

Just then the ball of pink yarn rolled off the sill and fell to the ground outside. The first wife seized a knife, cut off her hand and said:

"Go down. Bring me the wool."

When the hand had retrieved the ball of yarn, the first wife took the wool, reattached her hand and continued to weave.

That evening the second wife wanted a glass of water. She was thinking to herself: "Is she better than I am? No, I am as much the prince's wife as she is!" So she cut off her hand but before she could say, "Bring me a glass of..." her cries, loud as a bugle, could be heard beyond the palace roof.

The maid flew to her master yelling: "God keep you, Master! My mistress cut herself, she is bleeding rivers!"

On a third occasion the king's son said to the maid:

"Go to my first wife and tell her that your master fancies a cluster of grapes from her grape arbor."

The maid brought the message and the first wife said:

"Welcome to you and your master."

First, she called to the basket, "Come!" And the basket stood before her. Then she pointed to the window: "Open!" And it swung open. Then she chose the most beautiful bunch of grapes and commanded it to fall into the basket, the basket to return inside, and the window to shut. Just so: she pointed her finger and gave her orders while she remained seated where she was.

She handed the basket to the maid saying:

"Take it and good health to you and your master!"

The maid carried the grapes to her master and repeated to him all that she had witnessed. The second wife was listening. She wished to imitate her rival but not one thing obeyed her: not the basket, not the window, not the grapes. When she climbed onto the arbor to pick some grapes herself, she fell and broke a leg. The maid ran inside shouting:

"God keep you, Master. My mistress's bones are broken! She is all in splinters!"

At last, one day the king's son confided in his friend telling him everything that had been happening. The friend had advice to give and the king's son listened. He went secretly into his first wife's palace and hid where he could spy on her. How great was his surprise when he heard her speak! He was even more surprised when he heard her say she that she was thirsty and saw a clay pitcher and a small water jar speeding to her side.

"Go to the spring," she ordered. "I am thirsty and want a drink."

Off they went! And when they were filled with water, they raced back, each vying to be the first to reach her. But the jar tripped and fell onto the pitcher's protruding spout and snapped it off. The pitcher burst into tears.

"Why are you crying?" asked the first wife.

"The jar fell onto my spout! She broke it off!" sobbed the water jug. "What am I good for now?"

"I neither fell nor broke anything," countered the jar. "It was the pitcher's doing; he stumbled and fell against a stone."

"Mistress, believe me!" said the pitcher, "I swear by the Sun your mother and the Moon your father that it was the jar's fault. It was she who broke off my spout!"

"That settles it, Jar, it must have been your fault," said the first wife.

Her husband did not wait to hear the end of their argument; he stepped out of his hiding place and said to his wife:

"I swear by the Sun your mother and the Moon your father that I have waited too long for you to speak! Talk to me, please."

When she heard these words, the first wife ran to her husband's side. He kissed her and she kissed him.

And they lived happily year after year.
God sweeten the days of the listeners here!

A HOUSE WITHOUT WORRIES

My back is bent
My strength is spent,
My mind is gone
My days are done,
The end is near
Lay me on a wooden bier,
Let the worms have good cheer.

THEY SAY, THOUGH GOD alone is All-Knowing, that there was an old woman whose back was bent and strength was spent. Her mind was gone and her days were done. She was close to death and the worms awaited her.

The old woman was worn out and exhausted; she was unable to fall asleep. Night after night she tried but it was no use. She said to herself that what she needed was to find a home untouched by worries or cares; in such a peaceful place she would be able to sleep. She knocked on her neighbor's door and asked:

"Do you have any worries, my child?"

The neighbor answered:

"I have worries above me and below me, Aunt; I am crushed by worry!"

The old woman knocked at another neighbor's door:

"My child, do you have any worries?"

"'To each as much worry as he can carry,' none of us is free of care," sighed the neighbor.

Wherever the old woman knocked at a door she would hear complaints and laments and weeping.

That is, until she reached a certain house where she asked her question and the woman inside said:

"Worry? What does that mean?"

"Yes!" the woman cried, "'The camel driver knew where to make a halt,' as they say." And she explained how she was searching for a house untouched by care where she could rest for a while and get some sleep.

"You are welcome!" said the young woman and invited her in, offering her food and hospitality. Then, after gathering some twigs into a bundle, she waited for her husband's return.

When the husband came home in the evening, they all sat down together, eating and drinking and talking. As soon as they had finished their meal, the husband took up the bundle of twigs and fell upon his wife, beating her with one switch after the other, saying:

"Where is the pain you feel?
I'll surely help you heal.
This lash will flay you
This one will slay you
And this will make you fall
And crack your skull against the wall."

With each blow he would ask her a question and she would answer him:

"Is there anyone pleasanter than I am?"

"No."

"Is there anyone handsomer than I am?"

"No."

"Is there anyone cleverer than I am?"

"No."

"Is there anyone wealthier than I am?"

"No."

When he'd used all the switches, the husband turned on his heel and left the house. The wife picked herself up and gathered the twigs into a bundle again. The old woman said:

"Such a beating, my child, and yet you claim you have no troubles! Why does he do it?"

So the woman told her:

"One day my husband brought home some grapes: a bunch of white grapes and a bunch of black ones. I said: 'How beautiful the black grapes look lying on top of the white.' From that moment he began to beat me every day. He must have interpreted my remark with some meaning of his own."

The old woman advised her:

"Listen to me, my child. If you want your husband to stop this ritual, the next time he asks his questions, say 'Yes! There is!'"

"And what if he asks who it is?" said the woman.

"Just tell him it is Shah Bandar of the Merchants," said the old woman. Then bidding her goodbye, she continued on her way.

On the following day the young woman set out the bundle of switches as usual. After they had eaten their supper the husband began to beat her:

"Do you still feel sore?

Here's my cure once more.

This blow will flay you

This one will slay you,

This one will split your head

And fill you full of dread."

With every stroke he asked his usual questions but she did not give her usual answers:

"Is there anyone pleasanter than I am?"

"Yes, there is!"

"Is there anyone handsomer than I am?"

"Yes, there is!"

"Is there anyone cleverer than I am?"

"Yes, there is!"

"Is there anyone wealthier than I am?"

"Yes, there is!"

This drove her husband mad. He stopped short and shouted:

"If there is such a one, who is he?"

"Shah Bandar of the Merchants," replied his wife.

All that night the husband lay awake and could not sleep. Early the next morning he started out in search of this man. He traveled through many parts, up one country and down the next; "one place lifted him and another set him down," as they say. At last he came to a walled city. There he saw a carriage inlaid with corals and pearls. He asked the people around him who owned such a costly carriage. They said:

"It belongs to Shah Bandar of the Merchants!"

"I have come to the right place!" said the husband to himself. "This is the very man I am after!"

He followed the carriage until it stopped in front of a palace. There he waited on Shah Bandar of the Merchants, introducing himself and greeting him. He said that he had traveled a long way to come and tell him a story. Shah Bandar invited him to enter and asked what this story was. So the husband told his tale saying, "This and this and this happened and then she gave me your name."

Shah Bandar asked some questions:

"Is your wife beautiful?"

"Yes."

"Is your wife young?"

"Yes."

"Is your wife bright?"

"Yes."

So he gave the husband a comb made of ivory and said:

"Here is a present for your wife. She can comb her hair with it and wear it too."

The man returned to his wife, gave her the comb and said:

"He has sent you a gift."

The woman bathed herself and arranged her hair. But the instant she stuck the comb in her braid she felt a flutter and was lifted into the air. She flew and flew until she landed beside Shah Bandar of the Merchants. When Shah Bandar saw her, he cried out:

"Praise the Lord, Creator of such perfection!"

He welcomed the woman with open arms and asked her to be his wife.

Finding happiness in each other
And lived free of worry and bother.
A long life of contentment and ease
That blessed them with all things that please.

THE PRINCE AND THE GOATHERD

Let us begin by saying
There is no God but God.

THERE WAS OR THERE WAS NOT, O gracious listeners, an Emir, a prince of the Arabs of the desert. He ruled over wide spaces and his subjects were many. Every day he stood at his window looking through a long telescope, wishing to observe his people. In this way he was aware of everything that occurred in his territory.

One day he noticed in the distance a hut that stood empty. He kept looking and saw that a man lived in it who was poor and whose only possession was a goat. Every morning the man went out with his goat, and his stick slung over one shoulder. Every evening he returned.

The prince wondered how the man was able to live in isolation from the world, owning nothing but this goat. He determined to take a closer look. One day he decided to disguise himself so that he could mingle with the people without being recognized and check on their welfare. Among the rest, he wanted to pass by the goatherd.

It took a long walk to reach the distant hut. The prince knocked on the door and introduced himself as a wandering dervish. The goatherd received him and bid him enter saying:

"Welcome to you, O Dervish of the Blessings!"

The two men conversed and the prince discovered that the goatherd did indeed live by himself and that he owned nothing besides the goat. The goat's milk was his food and also some vegetables he grew in the ground nearby.

The dervish-prince began to feel thirsty and asked the goatherd for a drink. Immediately the man hurried to milk his goat and offer the dervish a drink of milk. After a while the prince felt hungry and asked the goatherd for something to eat. Quickly he slaughtered his goat, grilled the meat and offered it to the dervish to eat.

The prince was overwhelmed by the man's kind welcome and his generosity. He wanted to express his appreciation and his respect so he said:

"I am grateful to you for your hospitality. I don't know how to reciprocate. But take this letter and present it to the Emir of the desert Arabs. He lives in the town on the other side of the quarter and surely he will reward you."

With that the prince took his leave and returned to his castle.

The goatherd murmured to himself:

"Let me decide about the letter in the morning. As they say: 'Start early in the day to earn good pay.'"

But the next morning he felt hesitant about going to the Emir, thinking:

"To address a plea to any but God is debasing."

On the following day he had another thought:

"Why not go and try my luck?"

On the third day he woke up hungry. So he put his cap on his head and slung his stick across his shoulders and set out. He went walking and walking until he arrived at the Emir's town. There were crowds of people in the open square listening to the final words of a speech the Emir was giving:

"O my people! O my Tribe!

Let whoever wants sustenance seek it from God.

Do not ask for sympathy; do not ask for help from your fellows.

Go in peace and let each of you look to himself and God's mercy!"

When the crowd dispersed, the goatherd remained alone in the square pondering what the Emir had said, thinking: "How can I ask this man for anything after such a statement?" He tore up the letter, picked up his stick, and returned the way he had come.

He traveled a long way before he came to a wide river and sat down on the riverbank to rest. He began poking his stick in the water. Suddenly he found he could no longer move it; the stick had caught on something. He got up and pulled and pulled until he saw that the stick had hooked onto a ring attached to a large tin chest. He waded into the water and dragged the chest to shore. There he opened it and looked inside and could not believe his eyes. It held a rich treasure: piles of gold coins heaped together and glistening in the sunlight. The sight of such wealth restored the goatherd's energy. He jumped up, lifted the tin chest and carried it all the way back to the town. He cashed the gold, bought cattle and tents and returned to his own place. Now he was able to build himself a house, farm the land, and employ servants and attendants to work for him.

Days came and days went and the goatherd lived happily and in peace. Then one morning the prince looked through his telescope and saw that the goatherd's hut had become a house, his land was ploughed and planted, and he had numerous tents and herds of cattle. So once more he dressed himself as a wandering dervish and went to visit.

The goatherd greeted him saying;

"Welcome to the Dervish of Blessings! Welcome to the guest! Bring on the she-camels. Slaughter them in his honor."

The prince asked the goatherd to tell his story. So the man recounted how he used to live alone with his goat and how there came "a dervish just like your Grace," who proved that, in the end, all blessings and good fortune are from God. In his turn, the prince revealed who he was. He explained that he himself was the dervish who had called on him before and that he had been deeply touched when the goatherd slaughtered his goat to feed him. The men embraced and swore brotherhood to each other.

From then on, the prince's visits to the goatherd became more frequent and the goatherd was often the subject of the prince's conversation. This became a source of worry for the prince's vizier; jealousy consumed him and he began to fear for his position. He said to the prince:

"This man used to be a humble goatherd. Now that he has become a man of wealth, he is like an Emir. Beware of him!"

"I have no reason to doubt him," said the prince.

The vizier said:

"He may well be aiming to replace you. Is it not better to get rid of him rather than wait for him to depose you?"

The prince was uncertain but finally he said:

"What do you suggest?"

"This man is a Bedouin," said the vizier. "He can foresee the future, he is a seer. Ask him to interpret a dream for you and if his answer displeases you, cut off his head."

The prince summoned the goatherd and said:

"I have had a disturbing dream. In it a black dog barked into my face three times. Can you explain what that means?"

The vizier meanwhile sat nearby watching the goatherd from the corner of his eye, trying to hide a knowing smile.

"A black dog that growled three times?" asked the goatherd shaking his head. Then he said:

"With the first *grrr – ow – ow* the dog seemed to say 'glow' meaning: 'The candle will forever glow.'"

The prince understood the interpretation to be that he would continue to rule as Emir undiminished.

"With the second *grrr – ow – ow* the dog was saying 'grow' meaning: 'To the height of the tree the sapling will never grow.'"

The prince understood the goatherd to say that he would never usurp the Emir's title.

"With the third *grrr – ow – ow* the dog seemed to say 'woe' meaning 'God's curse on him who conspires to create woe.'"

The prince understood that the bringer of woe was the vizier himself who had been plotting the goatherd's downfall. He gave orders for the vizier to be executed and replaced him with the goatherd.

As for me – when I departed that place the Emir was still ruling his people with equity and justice.

LADY TANAQEESH AND
THE EGGS OF THE TAWAWEES

THERE WAS A MAN WHO LIVED with his three daughters. The name of the eldest was Dolaban, the middle daughter was called Shamlakan, and the youngest, Lady Tanaqeesh. The prettiest and brightest and most pleasant of the three was Lady Tanaqeesh, and her father loved her dearly. Naturally, her two older sisters were jealous of her:

"She gets the tastiest treats, the sweetest words, the morning smiles and goodnight kisses. Our father's affection is showered on her alone."

One spring day, the girls' father was preparing to go on a journey to Damascus. He asked his daughters what gifts they wanted him to bring back for them.

Dolaban said: "I want a wooden chest – a dolab."

Shamlakan said: "I want a woolen vest – a shamla."

And Lady Tanaqeesh said: "I wish you would bring me a dress with sleeves that clap and hems that dance."

Their father bid his daughters goodbye and departed. He was still away on his travels at Eastertide, the season for boiling eggs. People used to eat them on the day they call "Thursday of the Eggs" to ward off scabies.

It happened that on that day a peddler passed in front of the girls' house calling:

"Tawawees eggs for sale! Peacock eggs are what I'm selling!

They get a girl with child without a groom or wedding."

The two older sisters smiled. They understood each other perfectly. No need for words. Down they ran to the peddler and bought the eggs that bring on pregnancy. Then they called to the youngest sister:

"Lady Tanaqeesh, today it is your turn to look out for the wheat."

The wheat was spread on the flat rooftop of their house to dry in the sun and the girls took turns to guard it from the birds. The older sisters said:

"Lady Tanaqeesh, don't worry about your lunch. We'll bring the food up to you. Just watch the wheat so the birds don't get it."

The girl climbed up to the roof and sat down cross-legged to keep watch. All at once she saw two doves come flying towards her. She picked up a few grains of the wheat and offered them to the birds with outstretched palm. The doves pecked the wheat out of her hand and flew away.

Meanwhile Dolaban and Shamlakan were busy preparing the peacock eggs for their sister. They carried them, still steaming in the frying pan, up to the roof with a round of bread.

"Here is your lunch, Lady Tanaqeesh," they said. "Eat it in good health."

The girl thanked them and began to eat while her two sisters observed her closely. After one or two mouthfuls her belly began to swell. With the third mouthful it bulged even more. With each bite her belly grew bigger and by the time she had finished it had rounded out like a ball. The girl stood up and looked at herself in shock while her sisters screamed:

"What have you done to yourself?

What shall we tell your father?

'Our sister ate the eggs of a peacock,

Now she is pregnant out of wedlock?'"

The girl sat alone on the rooftop, asking herself: What had befallen her? How could she face her father? What was she to do?

One after another, the days passed until the father returned from his travels. He gave Dolaban the wooden chest and Shamlakan the woolen vest. Then he asked. "Where is Lady Tanaqeesh?"

"She is on the roof for the wheat that's out to dry," they said.

He repeated his question in the evening and they told him she was still with the wheat. When he asked for her the next morning, they broke the news to him that his daughter was pregnant and that she was living on the roof:

"Lady Tanaqeesh is pregnant, Father. She refuses to come down from the rooftop. We have to carry her food up to her!"

The father ran up the steps to the roof and with his own

eyes he saw his daughter's swollen belly. She tried to explain but he would not listen to one word out of her. He had decided that she must pay with her life. He intended to kill her but found he could not do it. So he called one of the huntsmen he knew and asked him to do the deed for him because he himself was unable to kill his daughter.

"Kill her and bring me her blood," he said.

The huntsman set off to carry out his task taking Lady Tanaqeesh with him. He led the way and she followed behind. They walked and walked until she was tired and had to stop for a rest. Exhausted, she leaned her head against a tree and instantly fell asleep. The huntsman raised his gun and aimed at the girl but he could not bring himself to kill her. Deciding that telling a lie was a lesser sin than taking a life, he said to himself:

"I'll give her father the blood of some small creature and tell him it is his daughter's blood."

The huntsman left the girl asleep and returned to her father with animal's blood as he had planned. He said:

"I have killed her. Here is her blood."

And Lady Tanaqeesh? She opened her eyes with the breaking light of dawn and found she was in a barren landscape with no idea in which direction she should go. She began to cry and went on crying until she heard a fluttering overhead. Looking up she saw a flock of pigeons circling above her. They seemed to be signaling that she should follow them. She began to walk, the birds flying ahead of her in the air while she ran after them on the ground, until she arrived in front of a small hut.

It was dirty inside so she cleaned it; it was untidy so she set it in order. She made everything ready to receive the child she was bearing. Finally, when the time came she gave birth to her infant in the hut. And after regaining her strength she went on living there with her little son.

One day she climbed onto the roof of the hut. From there she was able to see, in the distance, the top of her father's house. She saw that the wheat was still spread out on the roof. So she pointed the doves to the house and said:

"O my doves, my dear ones,
Look far away, over there, and see
My father's house by the poplar tree
A round window above the terrace on one side
On the rooftop wheat and barley spread out wide
Fly, my darlings, fly there and land on the wheat.
Eat all you can eat,
Scatter all you can scatter,
Spill all you can spill,
Carry off all you can carry
And be sure to sing your song."

The birds took off. They flew to the house of Lady Tanaqeesh's father and dropped down onto the roof. It was Dolaban, the eldest sister's turn to guard the wheat. "Shoo, birds, Shoo!" she shouted. But the doves pecked at the wheat and scattered it and spilled it and carried it off singing:

"We won't be shooed, we won't be chased

We are the doves of Lady Tanaqeesh

The one you shamed and you disgraced

Feeding her the eggs of the tawawees."

The eldest sister Dolaban ran to the middle sister, Shamlakan, asking her to help drive away the birds and keep them off the wheat. Shamlakan waved her hands, "Shoo, Birds! Shoo!" But the birds went on eating the wheat and scattering it and spilling it and carrying it off and singing:

"We won't be shooed, we won't be chased

We are the doves of Lady Tanaqeesh

The one you shamed and you disgraced

Feeding her the eggs of the tawawees."

The father inside the house could hear the noise and fuss on the roof and he saw grains of wheat falling outside. He called out:

"Dolaban, what are you saying?"

"Nothing, nothing!" she called back.

Then he shouted:

"Shamlakan, what are you saying?"

"Nothing, nothing!" she answered.

The father went up to the roof. He saw the girls, their hair in disarray, surrounded by the birds that were scattering wheat in all directions. So he too tried to chase them off crying:

"Shoo, pigeons! Shoo!"

The birds quieted down and said:

"We won't be shooed, we won't be chased

We are the doves of Lady Tanaqeesh

The one you shamed and you disgraced

Feeding her the eggs of the tawawees."

The father froze where he stood. But when the doves flapped their wings and began to fly up into the sky, he ran down, threw himself onto his horse and rode after them. The birds flew above while the horse followed below until the doves reached the hut where Lady Tanaqeesh was living with her child. The young woman had been looking out of the window so she saw the birds arriving and her father on horseback stopping in front of the hut and dismounting. Before he knocked at the door Lady Tanaqeesh quickly hid her son out of sight. The father knocked and called her name and when she opened the door he kissed her on her brow. After drinking some water and watering his horse and resting himself and his horse, he told her that he had learned the truth and said:

"I have come to take you home. Bundle up your clothes and come with me."

Lady Tanaqeesh tied up her clothes and rode with her father. When they had gone a little way she turned towards the hut behind her and said:

"Father, please! I have to go back. I have forgotten my thimble."

He said: "But you have a thimble at home."

She said that she liked this thimble, it fitted her finger perfectly, and she did not want to part with it.

So they turned back. The girl dismounted while her father waited outside. As soon as she entered the hut, Lady Tanaqeesh ran to her child, and lifted him into her arms. She nursed him, singing as she rocked:

"Nurse, nurse, my dear little son

Soon, soon your mother will be gone."

The child began to cry, his mother wept with him and so did the doves that had gathered around her. Then she kissed her son and charged the doves to take good care of him. She took the thimble and mounted the horse behind her father.

They had not gone very far when again she turned to look back at the hut and said:

"I beg you, Father, please stop. I left my spool of thread behind."

"But we have plenty of thread at home," he told her.

She said that this was strong thread, dyed a beautiful color; she liked it and did not want to part with it.

Back they went again. She dismounted and her father waited for her while she went into the hut. She picked up her son and kissed him. She nursed him, rocking and singing:

"Nurse, nurse, my dear little son

Soon, soon your mother will be gone."

The boy cried and his mother wept and so did the birds. Lady Tanaqeesh kissed her son and repeated her recommendations to the doves. Then she took the spool of thread and climbed onto her father's horse.

When she turned for the third time to look behind her at the hut, all she could see was part of the roof because by then they had traveled a little farther.

"Please, Father," she shrieked, "Father, I beg you, let me go back! I have forgotten my needle."

"But we have many needles at home," said her father. She stressed that this particular needle was sharp and easy to thread because it had a large eye.

For the third time they returned to the hut. The girl went inside. This time her father did not stay on his horse but dismounted and, keeping out of his daughter's sight, he walked carefully to window and peered through the opening. He saw everything! He saw Lady Tanaqeesh picking up her son to nurse him, rocking and singing:

"Nurse, nurse, my dear little son
Soon, soon your mother will be gone."

He saw how she wept and the child cried and how the doves around her also cried. He saw her kiss her son telling the birds to look after him.

The father retraced his steps and mounted his horse and waited for his daughter.

Lady Tanaqeesh came out with her needle and climbed

behind her father ready to go. But the horse did not move. The girl wondered why and her father said,

"A thimble, a spool of thread, and a needle: are you sure you have not left something else in the hut that you love and cannot be parted from?"

Lady Tanaqeesh made no reply. She remained silent, but tears were running down her cheeks. Her father said:

"Go, dear daughter! Go and bring the child you love and can't be parted from!"

The girl jumped off the horse, ran into the hut, and came out carrying the child in her arms. They rode home with the doves circling above their heads, keeping them company all the way.

Dolaban and Shamlakan both happened to be standing on the rooftop. When they saw Lady Tanaqeesh and her child riding home with their father, they were alarmed and went into hiding. But the father summoned all three daughters to come before him. Dolaban and Shamlakan were trembling with fright. The father said he wanted to hear from each of them what had happened. When he had listened to their stories from beginning to end, he said:

"Lady Tanaqeesh, how do you want to repay your sisters for what they have done?"

"I was waiting for my revenge," she replied, "I was wanting to say:

'Father, seize them by the hair and kill them one by one
Their guts will serve as ropes to hang my washing on,
Their skulls two bowls in which to keep the chicken's feed.
Then tear them limb from limb, their arms, their legs,
        their feet.
With their bones I'll build a ladder to reach the roof
Of their punishment it will be a solid proof.
Stepping on the ladder's rungs I'll hear their groans
Climbing up at every step I'll tell the bones:
'Creak! Creak!
Who started with these horrors?
Creak! Creak!
You and you were the aggressors!
Creak! Creak!
You and you were the oppressors!
Going down I'd tread hard on every rung and cry:
Creak! Creak!
Have I harmed you? No not I!
Creak! Creak!
Was I cruel to you? No not I!
Creak! Creak!
You were the evil ones and not I!
Yes, you both deserve to die!'"

Then she added:
"Now that I hold this darling boy in my arms I wish Dolaban

and Shamlakan to suffer only as I have suffered. Let them live in dishonor and disgrace, alone and far from the human race."

After that Lady Tanaqeesh married the huntsman who had spared her life and they lived peacefully without cares and had many children, both boys and girls.

THE OLIVE PIT

I do not dare to tell a lie
A lie could trip me by and by.
I can throw a saddle on a flea
I can ride it everywhere I please.
And when my flea swims in the sea
The water barely wets its knees.
I never want to tell a lie
A lie could trip me by and by.
I can pasture camels
Two thousand at a time
On one broad bean
That's fresh and green.
We cooked and filled a thousand pots
With half a bird, that's all that we'd got.
We fed Aleppo, Damascus, and Istanbul,
And still had meat enough to keep and cool.
I do not know how to tell a lie.

THERE WAS THIS WOMAN who was barren. She was unable to conceive or carry a child.

On the blessed night at the end of Ramadan, the month

of fasting, when wishes are granted, the woman prayed and prayed:

"Grant me the taste of motherhood, O Lord! Grant me an infant, a daughter that I can raise and love. Grant me a child, O Lord, even if it is a mere olive pit."

God heard the woman's prayer. She became pregnant and gave birth to an olive pit. With her olive pit in her hand she walked until she was outside the town. There, on the rise of a hill, she planted her olive pit and lovingly tended her. Every day she would go to visit her and recite nursery rhymes, sing children's songs, and tell her stories. Soon the olive pit grew into a tree. A child in a story grows fast. And one day, out of the trunk of the olive tree, there appeared such a girl... praise be to her Creator! The mother's heart swelled when she saw her. Now she was able to instruct and guide her. In time the woman grew old and died, but she was at peace knowing that she had done for her daughter all that was necessary.

The olive tree flourished and spread its branches thick and wide. People came and sat under it to cool off and enjoy the shade. When no one was about, Olive Pit emerged to gather the food that people left behind, drink some water from the river, pick flowers, and listen to the birds before returning to her tree.

One day the king's son passed by the hill and rested under Olive Pit's tree. He liked the spot. So his men pitched the tents and gathered in the leafy shade. The prince said to his cook:

"We are going hunting. Be sure to prepare a meal for us while we are away and have it ready for our return."

The royal cook prepared the food and spread it under the tree. As soon as he had gone to the tents, Olive Pit came out. From every dish she took one mouthful then quickly went back to her place inside the trunk of the olive tree.

When the King's son returned from the hunt, he saw that food was missing off every plate. He questioned the cook:

"Did you set out the dishes without filling them? Or did one of you taste my food before I did?"

"No! Never! God keep you, O Ruler of Our Time!"

The same thing happened on the second day of the hunt and on the third. So the king's son decided to hide and secretly spy on what was going on in his absence.

He saw how the trunk of the olive tree split open and that a graceful, slender girl stepped out to eat a mouthful off every plate. Just as she was about to disappear into the tree again, the prince stopped her, seizing her by the arm. He told her that he was the king's son and that he had been watching her. Who was she? What was her name? She said that she was Olive Pit, that her mother had died and she was living inside the tree.

The prince invited Olive Pit to dine with him. Food was brought and laid before them. They supped together that night and every night that followed. During the day Olive Pit hid in the tree and after sunset she spent her time with the prince. One evening the prince brought the young woman a gift: a bracelet of gold. He placed it on her wrist then kissed her arm. He invited her to dine as before, but this time, instead of returning to her tree after the meal, Olive Pit fell fast asleep where she sat. The prince decided this was the moment to slip away quietly with all his men. They did not wake the girl and left her sleeping.

Olive Pit woke up to find she was alone on the bare hillside. What had happened to the tents and pavilions? Where were the men? And where was the prince? Maybe she had dreamt it all. But there on her arm was the golden bracelet. "If only it was just a dream," she said to herself, "of tents and moonlit evenings and only a dream that my love has abandoned me and left!"

The girl was too unhappy to live as before. She started walking away from her tree and down the hill. She kept on walking until she came to a traveled path where she met a Bedouin riding his donkey. She stopped him and said:

"O Bedouin, Brother! Will you give me your clothes and your donkey in exchange for my bracelet of gold?" She thought to herself, "He can have the bracelet. I will keep the kiss."

The Bedouin agreed. So she dressed herself in the man's clothes and rode his donkey following the traces of the prince's party. When she caught up with the prince's men none of them recognized her. Even when she rode abreast of the prince's horse he did not know who she was. He said:

"Tell me about your adventures on the road, O Bedouin, our brother!"

She replied:

"I saw a young woman, not very old,
Her beauty a wonder to behold,
On her wrist a bangle of purest gold.
She was calling:
'O my love, O people's darling!
Lover of wine and glasses clinking
You left while I was sleeping.
Had I been awoken
A sweet farewell I would have spoken.'"

At these words the prince's eyes filled with tears. The "Bedouin" turned as if wishing to ride away but the prince chased after him and begged him to remain:

"Stay with me, my Bedouin friend! I am heading back to my own country and I wish you to be my guest for some days."

For the duration of the journey the two kept each other company. The prince never tired of hearing the Bedouin talk about the olive tree on the hill and how its shade fell like a tent on whoever stood below. Time and again he would turn the conversation to ask about the young woman of great beauty whom the Bedouin had seen wearing a bracelet of gold:

"Tell me, my dear traveling companion, what else did she say to you?"

Each time Olive Pit would give the same reply.

When they reached the prince's country there were crowds waiting to receive him.

"Why so much excitement?" she asked.

"They are making preparations for a big celebration, for a wedding, for my wedding. I am to marry my uncle's daughter. But I can set a room aside for you to use, my friend."

As the saying goes, "The sad one came to be happy and gay. She found this was no place for her to stay."

During the day Olive Pit would appear as the Bedouin and take her meals and converse with the prince. When evening came she joined the women and sang and danced with them as they celebrated: "Masked by daylight – her true self at night."

The prince began to wonder why he only saw his friend the Bedouin during the day and then with the onset of evening the man vanished. He was nowhere to be found, not even in the quarters they had set aside for him. The prince also noticed a young girl, slim and elegant, who sat among the women and danced and sang with them. Why did he see her only in the evenings and never by day? And why did no one know anything about her?

Here was a puzzle and he began to keep watch. With a shock it dawned on him that the Bedouin and the girl were one and the same person. He was filled with joy. He was elated. "This is Olive Pit!" he said to himself, "And I cannot live without her!" On the morning of the wedding day he went to see the cousin who had been promised to him in marriage. He told her his story from beginning end. She was saddened but she agreed that his was a story of true love.

The prince then went and seated himself next to the Bedouin and said,

"O Bedouin, our brother, a favor I beg:
If you see the young woman, not so old,
Who is a wonder to behold,
With on her wrist a bracelet of rarest gold
And you hear her calling:
O my love, O people's darling!
Lover of wine and glasses clinking!
Say to her, I beg:
Had I dared to wake her, I would have asked her then
If she would have me as her wedded husband,
In accordance with the laws of God and men."

Olive Pit smiled and tore off the Bedouin head cloth. She was beautiful to begin with, now she became more beautiful still. The prince held her to his heart.

> *They signed the marriage deed*
> *And placed it where all could see*
> *That here was a husband and his wife*
> *Bound by law and love for all their life.*

THE FLY

A FLY LANDED on a wall and said:
"Wall, Wall, how tall you are!"

"What use is that?" said the wall, "When I can be nibbled by a rat?"

So the fly flit over to the rat and said:

"Rat, Rat, what a mighty nibbler you are!"

"What use is that?" said the rat, "When I can be caught by a cat?"

The fly went to the cat and said:

"Cat, Cat, what a mighty catcher you are!"

"What use is that?" said the cat, "When I am no match for a beating stick?"

So the fly flew towards the stick and said:

"Stick, Stick, how mighty is the pain you inflict!"

"What use is that?" said the stick, "When fire can burn me like a wick?"

So the fly hovered over the fire and said:

"Fire, Fire, how mighty is your heat!"

"What use is that?" said the fire, "When water can drench me in one beat!"

So the fly went to the river and said:

"Water, Water, how mighty is your drenching!"

"What use is that?" said the water, "When a bull can swallow me, his thirst quenching."

So the fly landed on the bull and said:

"Bull, Bull, how mighty is your thirst!"

"What use is that?" said the bull, "When a knife may cut me first."

So the fly went to the knife and said:

"Knife, Knife, how mighty is your edge!"

"What use is that?" said the knife, "When the blacksmith can hammer me with his sledge."

So the fly went to the blacksmith and said:

"Blacksmith, Blacksmith, how mighty is your hammer!"

"What use is that?" said the blacksmith, "When death can take me away forever."

So the fly addressed death and said:

"Death, Death, how mighty is your taking!"

But there was silence. No one replied.

PEARLS ON A BRANCH

There was or there was not
In olden days that time has lost…
O you who like stories and talk
No story can be pleasing and beautiful,
Without invoking the Almighty, the Merciful.

THERE WAS A KING – there is no sovereign but God – and this king had a daughter. She was his only child and he liked to please her. So when the month for the pilgrimage to Mecca drew near, the king asked his daughter:

"Tell me what do you want me to bring you from the Hajj?"

She said:

"I want you to travel in safety and come home safely."

Whenever he saw her he said:

"Speak, child, what do you want me to bring you from the Hajj?"

And her answer always was:

"Your health and safety are all I want, Father."

Her nurse began to scold her:

"What is the matter with you? Ask for something you wish for! Tell him, 'I want Pearls on a Branch.'"

The girl wrote the nurse's words on piece of paper, put the paper in a box, and gave the box to her father so he wouldn't forget her request. The King kissed her goodbye and, taking his vizier with him, he set out on the Hajj.

When the two men had completed the rituals of the pilgrimage and were ready for the return home, their camels would not move but remained parked on their knees as if frozen in place. The men thought:

"Maybe the camels are thirsty and that is why they won't budge."

The animals were watered but they continued on their knees. The vizier said:

"Is there some errand that you have forgotten, your Majesty? Maybe that is why the camels are unwilling to travel."

When he heard this, the King remembered his daughter's request. He retraced his steps to buy his daughter's gift. At the first store he came to he asked:

"Do you have pearls on a branch?"

"Ask my neighbor," said the storekeeper.

He asked the neighbor and the neighbor said:

"Ask my neighbor."

So from store to store and neighbor to neighbor he went, asking the same question and receiving the same answer. The king was puzzled. There was an old man sitting by the side of the road and to him he recounted all that had happened and asked:

"What am I to do? My daughter is an only child! The camels won't move! Where can I buy pearls on a branch?"

The old man said:

"Pearls on a branch cannot be bought or sold! But may I show you how to get there? If I point to the place with my hand it will be cut off. If I signal with my eye it will be torn out. If we talk about it my tongue will be cut off."

"So what can we do?" asked the king.

The old man said:

"Buy me a water jar. I will walk ahead and you and your friend will follow me. When I reach the right gate I'll stumble and the jar will break. That is where you will find pearls on a branch."

The King bought the jar and he and the vizier walked behind the old man until he fell and the jar broke at the gate of a magnificent palace. The king and the vizier entered the gardens and knocked at the door. A serving man opened and the king said,

"I have come looking for pearls on a branch."

The servant left them and returned with a good-looking young man, who asked the king what he wanted. The king told him about his daughter's wish, explaining what had happened each time he asked where he might buy pearls on a branch. He handed his daughter's box to the young man. Now this handsome youth was the owner of the palace and a king in his own right. He opened the box and saw that his name was written on the paper inside. But he did not reveal to the king or the vizier that he himself was Pearls on a Branch, Lulu Bighsunu. Instead, he asked the king,

"What is your daughter called?"

"Her name is Husun Kamil, Loveliness Perfected."

"Is your daughter beautiful?" asked the youth and the father replied,

"She is loveliness perfected."

The young king, who owned the palace, ordered seven veiled girls, their faces completely covered, to be brought to him. He began to lift the veils, one by one, and as he uncovered the first beautiful face he asked:

"Is your daughter as beautiful as this?"

"No, she is more beautiful," the father answered.

The young man unveiled a second and a third face until he had shown all seven girls. The father repeated his answer each time: that his daughter was more beautiful, until he had seen all seven girls. Then the youth gave back the box to his guest after writing a note, which he placed inside. The father took the box and rejoined the pilgrim caravan with his camels that now were standing, and willing to move.

On the journey home the king asked the vizier:

"Tell me, my vizier, what do you think is in this box that the youth gave back to me?"

"Guessing will not reveal its contents, your Majesty," said the vizier.

"Then we will have to open it," said the king.

The king opened the box. He was expecting to find a gift for his only daughter. Instead there was a piece of paper and written on it:

> *Husun Kamil, Loveliness Perfected, you may drive*
> *a nail through your heart*
>
> *Lulu Bighsunu, Pearls on a Branch, will not be*
> *coming to sit at your hearth.*

In a flash the king understood and realized that the handsome youth himself was Pearls on a Branch. That was his name. Now he saw what his daughter was after and muttered to himself:

"She brazenly sent me to bring her a bridegroom! She wanted me to lead him to her with my own hand!"

He raged at the impropriety and his anger was terrible. He sent a messenger to his kingdom with the order that his daughter was to be locked up immediately in the palace of isolation. He did not wish to see her face on his return.

The messenger arrived with the king's instructions and both mother and daughter were confused. They tried to understand what was wrong but could not guess. The news spread throughout the kingdom. It was the talk on every tongue: "The King has locked up Husun Kamil, his only daughter."

Finally the king returned with his vizier and the people crowded round to congratulate him on completing the Hajj and on his safe return. He handed out right and left, the usual gifts of dates and henna and sandalwood and incense.

When all the well-wishers had departed, the king's wife asked:

"What is troubling you, dear husband? How can you lock up your only daughter for no good reason? You brought presents for everyone but not one gift for her?"

"Here is her present," said the king, "I will not hand it to her myself!" In the heat of his fury, he threw the box on the ground. He told his wife that he was on his way to order the executioner to cut off his daughter's head. Crazed with terror, she begged him to explain the reason for his anger. He reported what had happened to him on his journey and that Pearls on a Branch was the name of a young man whom their daughter wanted as her bridegroom. His wife made light of the cause for his agitation and persuaded him not to harm the girl. Then she took the box and went to Husun Kamil and repeated all that she had heard. The girl was astonished and thought:

"How can this make sense? Would I ever ask my father to bring me a bridegroom and lead him to me with his own hand?"

Then she opened her present and saw the message inside the box. So what her father had said was true! She read aloud:

> Husun Kamil, Loveliness Perfected, you may
> drive a nail through your heart
> Lulu Bighsunu, Pearls on a Branch, will not be
> coming to sit by your hearth.

"How dare he write such words!" she said and decided that

she had to respond, she had to provoke him in return. She told her mother:

"I can't sit idly here. I have to go."

Her mother tried to talk her into staying, telling her to listen and calm down.

"No! I want to leave right away!" the girl said again.

The mother insisted "No!" and the daughter insisted, "Yes!" In the end the girl said that she was leaving right away but promised to return. Her mother found comfort in the promise.

So Husun Kamil got ready: she picked out a set of her father's clothes and packed a saddlebag filled with money, then mounted her horse and rode off to find Lulu Bighsunu. It was a long journey before she reached his city. There she saw an old woman and asked whether she might lodge with her. The old woman took her in. Husun Kamil lived in her house and cared for the horse as well. Next she asked the old woman where the slave market was and where the palace of King Lulu Bighsunu was. She stained her face to darken it and went to the slave market and told the merchant there that she wanted to be sold to the palace as a serving girl.

"You may keep for yourself whatever price I bring," she said.

The merchant took her to the palace and offered her to Lulu Bighsunu's sister:

"God willing, you will be lucky with this new girl," he said.

"This one is better looking than any of the girls you have brought me so far!" said the sister and led Husun Kamil to join the other servants.

It was the custom in that palace that every night a different serving girl carried supper up to the king. That evening, because she was new, Husun Kamil was chosen for the task. With the supper tray in her hands she entered Lulu Bighsunu's chamber. He saw her standing in the doorway and every bone in his body melted. He told the girl to sit at the table and dine with him.

"Come sit and share my supper," he said.

She said:

"It is neither proper nor permitted for servants to eat at table with their masters."

He asked her to sit by his side at least. So she sat down. He chatted with her for a while then invited her to stay so they could play a game of chess after he had eaten. She agreed on one condition:

"Whoever of us wins will be allowed to tie the hands of the loser. What do you say?"

The king agreed, thinking to amuse himself. They played. She won. She tied his hands together and he spent the night like that, falling asleep with his hands cuffed.

The next evening he sent word that he wanted Husun Kamil to be the serving girl to bring him his supper. So she carried up the tray and sat with him and did as he asked. He wanted her to peel him an apple, which she did. But when she halved it she placed it on the palm of his hand and cut his skin as well as the apple with the knife. She begged forgiveness and quickly bound the wound with her kerchief.

He spent the night like that, falling asleep with the bandage around his hand. As for Husun Kamil, she fled to the old woman's house under cover of darkness, saddled her horse, and rode back to her own country.

Next morning, Lulu Bighsunu woke up to find Husun Kamil gone. He searched for her high and low, asking after her everywhere he went, but she was nowhere to be found. He breathed in her scent on the kerchief round his hand and kissed the bandage. As he did so, he heard the crackle of paper in the folded cloth. When he loosened the handkerchief and spread it out there was a letter hidden inside. He read:

> Lulu Bighsunu will not be coming to sit at
> Husun Kamil's hearth?
>
> The first night with her belt she tied your hands
> And let you sleep as if on firebrands.
>
> The second night she cut your palm and
> made it bleed
>
> You'll never be the one that Husun Kamil needs.

"Oh, what a trick!" he thought to himself, "But now I will show her!"

He went to the jeweler who worked in gold and commissioned him to sculpt a jeweled hen with all her chicks around her. He waited for the piece to be finished, then saddled up for travel and rode to Husun Kamil's country, taking with him the golden hen. Upon arriving in Husun Kamil's city, he made inquiries and learned that Husun Kamil was prisoner in the palace of isolation, living apart with only one woman, her nurse, to serve her.

Next morning, just as the sun was rising, Lulu Bighsunu stood below Husun Kamil's window, disguised as a peddler. He set down the jeweled hen where it would catch the sunlight.

"A jeweled hen, with all her chicks, for sale!" he called, "A hen of solid gold for sale!"

Husun Kamil's nurse looked out and saw something glittering in the sun.

"Mistress, come quickly! Come take a look!" she said.

The girl came running and saw the sunlight glancing off the gold. When the peddler turned a key, the jeweled hen moved, pecking and clucking. She looked again and recognized Lulu Bigshunu. She told the nurse:

"Ask how much he wants for his hen."

"How much does your hen cost?" asked the nurse.

"It cannot be bought for silver or for gold! My price is one night in your mistress's chamber," said the peddler.

"What? May fevers boil and burn you! How dare you even think about my mistress for a night?"

The nursemaid reported back to Husun Kamil what he had said. To her surprise, her mistress instructed her to tell him "yes." But on condition that it would be in the dark, in silence, in the room below the stairs. The maid went down to explain her mistress's conditions and the peddler accepted willingly. So the maid was able to bring the golden hen with all her chicks to Husun Kamil.

The plan was for the maid, and not her mistress, to be with Lulu Bighsunu in the room below the stairs. So Husun Kamil set to work on her nurse with kohl and powder, perfumes and essences. She warned her not to utter a single word to Lulu Bighsunu and gave her a letter to drop into his pocket before he left.

"Not a whisper, not a word!" she reminded her.

The maid went down to the room below the stairs and snuffed out the light. Lulu Bighsunu entered in darkness and spent the night below stairs thinking he was with Husun Kamil.

In the morning, feeling triumphant and happy, he left to travel back to his own parts. There, while he was changing his clothes, the letter fell out of his pocket. He read:

"Lulu Bighsunu you can drive a nail through your heart
Husun Kamil will not be coming to your hearth.
The first night with her belt she tied your hands
And let you sleep as if on firebrands.
The second night she cut your palm and made it bleed

You'll never be the one that Husun Kamil needs.
Now she owns your golden hen with chicks around
It was the slave girl with whom you slept so sound."

Stung and furious, Lulu Bighsunu resolved to take his revenge. He sent a messenger to her father asking for Husun Kamil's hand in marriage.

The father said:

"This requires deliberation. Let us think it over tonight and decide."

Since he was not talking to his daughter, her mother went to speak with her. The girl was willing and prepared herself for the journey to her husband's house. She asked her mother for three suits of her father's clothes, which her mother brought her along with two diamond pins, a gift from her father on this occasion. Husun Kamil packed the three sets of men's clothes, stuck the two diamond pins in her hair, and took the golden hen with her chicks and also a bag filled with small beads, both white and black. Then she set out for Lulu Bigsunu's palace to be wed.

When she arrived she was surprised to see the celebrations already under way. What was this? What did this mean? They told her:

"Lulu Bighsunu is celebrating the signing of the contract for his marriage to his first cousin, his paternal uncle's daughter."

Husun Kamil realized that Lulu Bighsunu's offer and his

intention had been to take her as his second wife, as co-wife to his first cousin.

In the evening Lulu Bighsunu summoned his Nubian serving man, Saiid, who loved him and served him loyally. Pointing to Husun Kamil he ordered him:

"You are to take Lady Husun tonight, Saiid. Take her and spend the night with her."

So on that first night it was Saiid who entered Husun Kamil's rooms. Husun Kamil meanwhile took out the bag of tiny black and white beads that she had brought with her and jumbled them. Then she said:

"Come, Saiid, sort out these beads. Separate the black beads from the white and when you are done, I'll be waiting for you inside."

She went into the inner room and Saiid sat, putting one black bead on this side, then one white bead on that. Long before the task was finished, he had fallen asleep.

Next day Husun Kamil called him, bid him good morning and said,

"Where were you, Saiid? I waited for you all night. But, come, take this suit of clothes with you to your master's bathhouse, have a wash, and put it on."

Lulu Bighsunu was in the bathhouse when Saiid entered. He asked:

"How was your night, Saiid?"

"As God is my witness, my Master, between black and white, I was up all night!"

"I wish you good health, Saiid! You have earned your keep."

On the second day Lulu Bighsunu again instructed Saiid to spend the night with Husun Kamil. What she did was break the lock on her door so it was impossible to repair. When it was evening, Saiid came in wanting to sleep. She said, "First lock the door, Saiid. When you are done, come; I'll be waiting for you."

So Saiid spent the night trying to mend the lock: pulling the hasp and pushing in the key, pulling and pushing without success. He tried and tried, but sleep overcame him before the job was done.

In the morning Husun Kamil called him:

"Good morning, Saiid. Where were you? I waited all night for you. But, here, take this suit and go to your master's bathhouse, wash yourself, and dress."

Saiid went to the bathhouse where Lulu Bighsunu was taking his bath. The king asked:

"How was your night, Saiid?"

"By God, it was push and pull, push and pull, hour after hour, my Master."

"Good work, Saiid! God grant you the best of health!"

On the third day, when Saiid came to Husun Kamil in the evening, she told him:

"This is the third and last night, Saiid. If you don't come to me this time, you will have to go back and sleep with the other servants."

During the day she had drilled holes in the bottom of the jar that held the drinking water. She said:

"Take this jar down to the well and fill it to the brim. When it is full, come to me; I'll be waiting."

So Saiid spent the night filling the bucket from the well and emptying it into the jar that had holes in the bottom. Again and again he'd fill the bucket with well water and empty it into the jar. When dawn broke, he was fast asleep and the water jar was still empty.

In the morning Husun Kamil called him, complaining:

"Really, Saiid! Was it right, the way you left me on my own waiting for you all night?"

He excused himself,

"I was busy, my Mistress, filling and emptying, filling and emptying."

She replied:

"Take this suit and go bathe in your master's bathhouse."

Saiid went to the bathhouse and when his master asked him about his night with Husun Kamil, he answered:

"By God, I had to keep at it, emptying and filling, emptying and filling, through the night."

"Bravo, Saiid! You have worked hard for your pay!" said the king.

That same morning Husun Kamil placed the golden hen with her chicks in the sunlight where Lulu Bighsunu's wife, his first cousin, could not miss it. She turned the key and the woman was delighted to see how the golden hen glittered and moved. The first cousin said:

"O wife of Saiid, will you let me have this treasure?"

"This is valuable jewelry, my Mistress, how can I give it to you?"

"What does it cost?" said the woman, "Tell me and I will manage it."

"It cannot be bought for silver or for gold," said Husun Kamil, "My price is a night with your husband the king. I will sleep one night with the king and you can sleep with Saiid."

"But what shall I tell my husband?" asked the woman.

"Say you want to try the Hammam of the Plants, the bath-house that restores to wives their maidenhood. And tell him also that after such a bath women have to spend the night in silence without talking. Your husband has to know that too."

The cousin ran to her husband, Lulu Bighsunu, and said,

"O King of our Time, there is a botanical bathhouse that will give back to women their maidenhood. What do you think? Should I go and bathe there?"

"Go! Of course! Go today; don't wait 'til tomorrow."

"But after such a bath," continued his wife, "I have to spend the whole night in silence without speaking a word to you."

Lulu Bighsunu agreed and waited for night to fall. That evening the king's wife went to spend the night with Saiid. He was happy – as happy as his name, "Saiid," which means "happy." There were no beads to sort, no mending of locks or filling of jars with well water. Meanwhile Husun Kamil went quietly into Lulu Bighsunu's room. It was pitch dark, she spoke not a word and he did not know that she was not his wife.

"I have a present for you," he said and slipped a gold bracelet onto her wrist. He told her that she was right, that indeed there was something different about the Hammam of the Plants and that he liked the effect. He encouraged her to use that bathhouse every day. After that they both fell asleep.

Before daybreak the next morning, Husun Kamil crept out of Lulu Bighsunu's bed and ran to Saiid's room where the king's wife was sleeping soundly, her arms around the serving man's neck.

"Wake up, O Cursed One," she said. "Wake up! Go back to your own house!"

It was the will of the Almighty that after this night both women should carry: the first wife, a child fathered by Saiid, and Husun Kamil a child by Lulu Bighsunu.

Then war broke out, and the king was forced to join in the fighting. Five years passed before the battle ended and he was able to return to his kingdom and his family. In his absence his wife had given birth to a boy who resembled Saiid and Husun Kamil to a boy who looked like himself. Ahead of the army's return, the king sent a messenger announcing the day of his arrival so that his people could prepare a welcome. He ordered them to have his son greet him on horseback with Saiid's son standing by, holding the horse's reins.

On the day of the soldiers' return, Husun Kamil put on the gold bracelet that the King had given her during the night. She took the two diamond pins, her father's gift, and fastened one in the hair of her son, who was holding the horse's reins, and the other in her own hair.

The king arrived with his army to welcoming crowds of people. When he saw the two boys, one on horseback and the other holding the reins, he assumed that his orders had been disobeyed. Annoyed by this, he demanded:

"Why did you switch the boys?"

He was told:

"God keep you, O King of our Time! The one on horseback is your son and the other is Saiid's."

The King was surprised by their words but he yielded to persuasion, remembering the saying, "Anger begins with madness and ends in regret."

One day, Lulu Bighsunu noticed among his wife's possessions the golden hen with all her chicks. He asked:

"How did you get this treasure?"

"Will you grant me immunity if I speak, your Majesty," she pleaded.

The king assented so she told him how she had slept that

night with Saiid while Husun Kamil had slept with the king: That had been the price of the treasure. The king said nothing. He did not know whether to be angered or delighted. But he hurried to Husun Kamil to ask for her side of the story. He said that his wife had confessed openly to what had taken place. So Husun Kamil told him all that had happened to her from the beginning to the end. Then she smiled and said,

"God keep you and grant you a long life, O King of our Time! Who ever heard of a Hammam of the Plants that can change women back to being maidens?"

And so Lulu Bighsunu married Husun Kamil. The wedding was celebrated and, having found each other, Pearls on a Branch and Loveliness Perfected lived happily to the end of their days.

The bird has flown,
It's time to go home!

TWO SISTERS

This happened… maybe it didn't…
Come sit with us and listen.
First we'll speak
Then we'll sleep.

A PRINCE LIVED in a palace magnificent
As befits the son of a king munificent.
His clothes were costly
His rooms were lofty
The chair he sat on, a gilded throne
The bed he slept in, of brass that shone.

Whenever the prince went hunting, he passed nearby the tents of a tribe of Bedouins. And every time he rode by, his eyes were fixed on Zuhayra, the girl of astonishing beauty who lived there.

Her robe was rough and wide
She pastured cattle for her tribe
The cup she drank from was metal – cheap but sound
The bed she slept in, straw matting on the ground.

Yet the king's son yearned for beautiful Zuhayra and longed to marry her. To his mother he confessed:
"I want to get married!"

"This is the moment we have been waiting for!" was her happy response. "Whom does your heart desire? Is it your Uncle's daughter or your Aunt's, or the daughter of our neighbors?"

To each question he answered "No!" and "No!" and finally he said:

"I want the Bedouin girl, Zuhayra! I have loved her from the instant I set eyes on her."

His mother shrieked in alarm:

"A prince, a king's son, marry the daughter of gypsies? We invite royalty to our weddings. What will they say about us then?"

When the youth explained that he would marry only the one his heart had chosen and no other, his mother relented. She made her way to the Bedouin tents and asked for Zuhayra's hand in marriage. And that is how the prince, her only son, was wed.

Now Zuhayra had a sister called Safiyya who had married a Bedouin youth. He lived in the tents of another tribe that eked out a living picking carob to make molasses and feeding its cattle with what was left. Safiyya lived with her husband as happily as when she was at home with her own people.

One day the father of the two sisters said to his wife:

"I feel like going to pay our daughters a visit to see how they are doing. What do you think, dear wife?"

The woman agreed and prepared provisions for his journey. The man set out at the crack of dawn, for the road was long and tiring. He was hungry and thirsty by the time he reached the king's magnificent palace. His daughter Zuhayra ran towards him when she saw him, high-heeled slippers clacking on the marble floor, rich clothing rustling as she moved. She bid him enter and straightaway summoned her servants and attendants with instructions:

"Clean him up! Give him proper clothes to wear! Make him look respectable!"

And so the father found himself stripped of his flowing robe, standing naked. Then he was bathed and dressed in tailored clothes, tight-fitting, uncomfortable. His feet were trapped in laced-up shoes. Zuhayra gave further orders:

"Spread the table! Serve the honey and the cream!"

Her father was used to sitting cross-legged on the floor; as best he could, he perched himself on a chair. He tried to catch a drink from water spouting out of a glass ewer. He did not know how: so he chose not to drink. To Zuhayra he said:

"I never eat in the mornings, dear child. My coming here is simply to check on you and to reassure your mother about you. Now that I have come and seen you, I can go and tell your mother how you are."

Zuhayra tried to give her father some money for her mother but his pride was hurt and he refused.

"Take her a little food, at least!" she said.

He would not accept any food either. Then he kissed Zuhayra goodbye and continued on his way to visit his other daughter.

He found Safiyya sitting in the shade of a goat hair tent. She welcomed her father joyfully and bid him sit beside her on the ground. She set before them two bowls: one with carob pods and the other filled with water. This was their meal: one bite of carob and then a sip of water to soften it and release its sweetness. The father dined on carob, sipped from the common drinking bowl and felt content. Before he left, Safiyya packed some carob pods for her mother. Then, bidding his daughter goodbye, the man returned to his wife.

"Tell me, how are the girls, how did you find them?" she asked.

He said:

"Zuhayra lives in unease and confusion,
Surrounded by great wealth and profusion.
Sweet honey is her food; her drink from a bubbling jug.
In high-heeled clogs she steps on marble floors and
    Persian rugs."

"What about Safiyya?" asked his wife.

He said:

"Saffiyya has married into a tribe modest and good
Plain water their drink, wild carob their food."

Both parents felt at peace and satisfied about their daughter Safiyya. As for Zuhayra, they wished her husband enlightenment and guidance from God.

There is no more to say
Good night to you and good day.

O PALACE BEAUTIFUL!
O FANCY FRIEND!

We went to Damascus and what did we see,
An old woman with skirts lifted high above her knee
Her buttocks were bare and of colors three:
Like grape, like pomegranate and mulberry!

O you who sit listening to what I say
There was, or was not, in a bygone day,
A man living with his daughter and his wife
In a modest house suited to their kind of life.

NOW THIS HOUSE WAS UNUSUAL and unlike any other. It was built by one of the Jinn. Onto the roof he had added a special room, a bathhouse with water running through it. But of this the husband had no knowledge.

Whenever the husband left the house to go to work, his wife took advantage of his absence and climbed up to the bathhouse on the roof. There she would soak herself in the perfumed water and look into the mirrors on the surrounding walls. She would breathe in the sweet scents and wait for the demon to appear. When he came he would bathe her and sit with her and entertain her with his talk. Then he would clothe the tips of her ten fingers with gold. Before leaving and going down to her home, she would look around her and ask:

"O Palace Beautiful! O Fancy Friend!
Is there anyone like me in the land?"
And the answer would be:
"No, not here nor anywhere on earth,
Is there a woman of comparable worth!"
This would please her and make her laugh. Then she would
go down to welcome her husband. And whenever her husband
returned and found her after her ten fingers had been tipped
with gold he was more delighted with her than before.

The daughter living in the house was a young girl of great
beauty and her name was Pomegranate-Seed-on-a-Platter. She
could hear what was going on around her but she had not seen
anything and barely understood the half of it. As she grew
up she listened more carefully to the voices and the talk; she
began to keep a watch on her mother; eventually she grasped
the exact words of the conversations she had been hearing.

One day when her mother was out, Pomegranate-Seed-on-
a-Platter decided to get the ladder and climb to the roof herself.
She discovered the room up there and she saw the water and
the mirrors; she could smell the sweet perfumes. As she lowered herself into the water, the demon made his appearance.
He bathed her and sat with her and entertained her. Then he
clothed the tips of her ten fingers with gold. She felt that something in her had changed. And she was happy.

When she went down into the house again she put everything back in its place. And, to hide her golden fingertips, she

put on a pair of gloves. Her father came home and they all sat down to eat. Her mother noticed the gloves and asked:

"Why are you wearing gloves at the supper table?"

The girl said nothing and when her mother repeated the question a second and a third time she did not answer.

The mother became suspicious. She could hardly wait for the moment her husband left the house. Next morning when he went to his work she hurried up to the roof and stepped into the water taking pleasure in her bath. When the Afreet had bathed her and sat and talked with her and clothed her ten fingers with gold, she asked:

"O Palace Beautiful! O Fancy Friend!

Is there anyone like me in the land?"

The answer came:

"Yes, in all honesty,

And she lives in this city."

She asked:

"Is that possible? Who can it be?"

The demon said:

"It is your own dear daughter

Pomegranate-Seed-on-a-Platter.

I bathed her, sat with her and entertained her.

I clothed her ten fingers with gold!"

The woman was stunned. She rushed down to her daughter and demanded to know why she had gone up to the bathhouse on the roof. The girl said:

"I wanted to see with my own eyes what my ears had heard."

The woman realized that she was at risk. She made no comment in answer to her daughter's words. She was saying to herself that her daughter had not only discovered her secret but had also become her rival. She called a driver who had a cart and horse and said:

"I'll pay you a handsome sum if you do as I tell you and do it on the quiet."

He said:

"What is it you want of me?"

She explained:

"Take Pomegranate-Seed-on-a-Platter somewhere far and kill her. Then bring back her blood for me to drink."

The man set out to do as he was told. He drove with the girl until he came to the edge of a dense wood. He asked her to stay there and wait for him. But as he stepped away he looked back and seeing how she stood and waited, trusting him completely, he felt pity for her. "I cannot commit murder," he was saying to himself. "God will look after her." In that moment a gazelle leapt out of the thicket and the driver killed it. He poured its blood into a glass jar that he gave to the girl's mother, saying her daughter was dead and here was her blood.

The father kept asking where his daughter was and his wife kept answering that she was with the neighbors or had gone here or gone there.

As for Pomegranate-Seed-on-a-Platter, she waited and

waited for the driver and eventually realized that he was not returning. So she started to walk in the direction of the city. She made her way through woods and thorns and tangled brambles until the blood was all but flowing from her feet. While she was wandering in this way, Ali Baba and his forty thieves caught sight of her. They began by arguing and quarreling about who among them should marry her. Then they saw the blood dripping from her feet and asked her to tell them her story. When she had finished her account of all that had happened they said:

"You shall be a sister to us!"

They took her to the cave that was their home and let her wash herself and gave her fresh clothes to wear. They offered her food and drink and she cleaned up their house. She lived there with them like a sister: cooking for them every day and waiting for them to come back in the evening from their work as highway robbers. They brought her fine and costly garments. For her part, she was content and happy to be living with the men in the cave.

Meanwhile, her mother continued to take her bath on the roof with the Afreet. Once when she asked:

"O Palace Beautiful! O Fancy Friend!
Is there anyone like me in the land?"

He said:

"Yes, I can say it to your face,
There is such a one in this place."

"Who is it?" she demanded.

He said:

"It is your own dear daughter
Pomegranate-Seed-on-a-Platter!
She is living, as if their sister,
With forty thieves and Ali Baba the robber."

The woman was mad with anger. She thought and thought and came up with a diabolical solution. She persuaded an old woman to go to Ali Baba's cave and pretend that she was an apple seller. For this she gave her a basket filled with apples. These were no ordinary apples; she had stuffed them with sharp iron nails. The old woman took the basket and waited near the cave until Ali Baba and the forty thieves went out. When Pomegranate-Seed-on-a-Platter was alone the old woman approached her:

"May God give you good fortune, child! Can you give me a sip of water?"

The girl bid her welcome and handed her the water jar. The old woman thanked her and offered her an apple before she left. As soon as Pomegranate-Seed-on-a-Platter bit into the apple for her first mouthful, the nails inside cut into her and she fell to the ground in a faint.

The young men returned to the cave and were shocked to see their adopted sister stretched out motionless on the ground with no sign of life. They wept and mourned her. They said:

"Our hearts will not permit us to bundle her into a shroud! Nor can we bear to dig a grave and bury her in the ground!"

So they placed her in a wooden chest and loaded the chest onto the back of a camel. Ali Baba gave the camel instructions:

"Take her, O camel, and carry her away! God's earth is spacious. But do not lower your neck and do not bend your back, unless you are commanded with the words: 'In the name of what is on your back!' Only then may you kneel and rest on the ground."

The camel left and traveled with his load until he was in the sultan's country. The sultan observed the camel crossing his territory with a wooden chest on its back. He wondered why a camel was wandering alone without a rider and he was curious about the contents of the chest. He approached the camel and shouted:

"Down, Camel!"

The camel stopped. It lifted its head high and did not move. This puzzled the sultan. He ordered the camel again:

"Bend your head, Camel!"

But the camel continued to stand without moving. Finally the sultan said:

"In the name of what is on your back, kneel, O Camel!"

The camel lowered itself gently and the sultan was able to reach for the wooden chest and open it.

Inside he found lying full length a young woman beautiful as the rising sun: her skin silken, her complexion pearls. He lifted her up and carried her to his palace. He laid her on his own bed and sat by her and wept and wept and wept until he had no tears left. He wept and wept until his mother came and remonstrated:

"My dear Son, this is not right! Let me wash her so that we may bury her."

So the sultan's mother began to wash the girl. While she was wiping her face she felt a nail protruding from her lip and pulled it out. In that instant the girl opened her eyes, looked around her and asked where she was. She also said that she was hungry.

The sultan's mother quickly went to call her son and bring him the happy news that the girl he had rescued from the chest on the camel's back was alive and well. Hardly believing his ears, the sultan ran to see her for himself. He was delighted when he saw her. He asked her her name and she told him that it was Pomegranate-Seed-on-a-Platter and went on to narrate her whole history. He loved her and asked her to marry him; she loved him and agreed to be his wife. So the feasts and celebrations began. Pomegranate-Seed-in-a-Platter invited Ali Baba and his forty thieves, for the sultan had pardoned them. All the people in the city were told to attend, and that for seven days no one was to eat or drink except as the sultan's guest.

When Pomegranate-Seed-on-a-Platter's mother heard that the sultan was holding a feast to celebrate his wedding she had no idea who the bride was. She began to get ready for the festivities and climbed up to the bathhouse on the roof. She went into the water and splashed perfumes on herself. The Afreet bathed her and sat with her and entertained her then clothed her ten fingers with gold. She asked:

"O Palace Beautiful! O Fancy Friend!
Is there anyone like me in the land?"
The demon answered:
"Yes there is, in all honesty
There is such a one in this city."
"Who can it be?" She asked.
He said:
"It is your own dear daughter
Pomegranate-Seed-on-a-Platter
Tinkling with golden jewels upon her
She's now the Sultan's wife, our ruler."

The woman was enraged; she was so furious that she was unable to breathe; hatred choked her and she burst and died.

But the young couple lived happily together
Until death took one and then the other.

WHO ATE THE WHEAT?

Climbing up the wall
Climbing down the wall
Your belt is tight, your waist is neat
If you want to know who stole the wheat
Listen to the story of Hee-Haw's Pond:

THERE ONCE WAS A FARM where a rooster, a goose, a dove and a duck were living together. With them there also lived a donkey.

One day the birds and the donkey decided to plant some wheat. Each of the birds carried a grain of wheat in his beak and dropped it to the ground. One grain at a time, the rooster, the goose, the dove and the duck sowed their whole field. Next, the birds shuttled back and forth, sprinkling water on their seeds. As each grain was moistened, it swelled and pushed out a small sprout. Back and forth, the birds took turns, coming every morning to water their wheat and tend it. Soon green shoots appeared above the ground. Then, day by day, they grew tall and ripened.

One night the donkey was feeling hungry. There before him stretched the new wheat. It made his mouth water. He took a bite. Then he took another and another until he had eaten it all.

The next morning it was the dove's turn to do the daily work. When she saw that the field was bare she quickly flew back to her friends, the other birds, and questioned them:

"Which one of you ate the wheat?"

The birds began to quarrel and accuse one another until the rooster suggested:

"Let us each fly across the pond. And may whoever ate the wheat fall into the water because of the weight in his belly."

Standing at the edge of the pond, the rooster crowed:

"Cock a doodle doo!

I am Rooster, listen all of you,

Only grapes I eat, as raisins too.

So let me sink in the water deep

If I am the one who ate the wheat."

Then the rooster took off and flew to the other side of the pond.

Next came the dove and said:

"Coo! Coo!

I am Dove, gentle and quiet,

Nuts and chickpeas are my diet.

So let me sink in the water deep

If I am the one who ate the wheat."

And the dove took off and flew to the other side of the pond.

The goose came next and said:

"Honk! Honk!

I am Goose who flies up high

My food is rice both boiled and dry.

So let me sink in the water deep

If I am the one who ate the wheat."

Then the goose took off and flew to the other side of the pond.

Next the duck said:

"Quack! Quack!

I am Duck with fat and wagging tail

I eat grains out of the farmyard pail.

So let me sink in the water deep

If I am the one who ate the wheat."

And the duck took off and flew to the other side of the pond.

It was the donkey's turn but he was gone.

The rooster gave a shout:

"Come, Donkey, come and prove your innocence as we did."

"I'm coming," said the donkey, "first I want to kick up my heels a couple of times."

He kicked up his heels and kicked and kicked but did not come.

The dove said to him:

"Come, Donkey, come and prove your innocence as we did."

"I'm coming," said the donkey, "first I want to bray a couple of times."

He brayed and brayed and brayed but he did not come.

The goose yelled:

"Come, Donkey, come and prove your innocence as we did."

"I'm coming," said the donkey, "first I want to flick my tail once or twice."

He flicked his tail and flicked and flicked but he did not come.

The duck called out:

"Come, Donkey, come and prove your innocence as we did."

"I'll come," said the donkey, "after I run up and down this open ground."

He ran and ran and ran, but still he did not come.

Then the birds, the rooster, the goose, the dove, and the duck – all shouted together:

"Where are you, Donkey? Come!"

This time the donkey came and stood by the pond. He said:

"Hee! Haw!

I am Donkey, stand aside let me pass,

My only meal is fresh, green grass.

So let me sink in the water deep

If I am the one who ate the wheat."

Then he leaped up and fell into the middle of the pond.

"Serves you right!" the birds all cried.

And from that day the pond has been known as Hee-Haw's Pond.

THE VEGETABLE-SELLER'S DAUGHTER

Peace be upon the soul of the Prophet,
And Jesus and Moses, Peace upon them.
If any here be burdened by sin, let them ask God's
forgiveness!

THERE WAS A KING – though none is sovereign but God –
and this king had a son, his only child. He taught the boy
to read and write and raised him in the manner of kings.

In a modest house next to the king's palace lived a vegetable
seller and his daughter. One day as the king's son was walking
out from the palace he took a long look at a beautiful young
woman sitting at her window. He knew she was the grocer's
daughter and that she sat there every day because he saw her
every time he passed by the grocer's house. The king's son
greeted her:

"Good morning, O Vegetable-Seller's Daughter."

"Good morning Prim Princeling," she responded, "future
son-in-law of my father!"

The young man was shocked by the way she addressed him.
The girl's boldness had startled him. In a mocking and haughty
voice he said:

"Is a son of the sultan to marry a grocer's daughter?"

"They say: 'He who keeps company with tramps becomes
their equal,'" she retorted.

The young man went on his way, upset and disturbed. How dare she address him in that tone! How dare she say such things! He was, after all, the king's son. Was he, a prince, to be her father's son-in-law? Nevertheless, all through the day, the greengrocer's daughter chased every other thought out of his mind. Her image was in his eyes, her voice in his ears, and her words in his head. The king's son was mightily annoyed.

When he returned to the palace that evening, he passed by the greengrocer's house and saw the girl again. He said:

"Good evening, O Vegetable-Seller's Daughter!"

She smiled and answered:

"Good evening, Prim Princeling, future son-in-law of my father!"

The young man laughed at her:

"Would a sultan's son ever marry a greengrocer's daughter?"

She said:

"He who keeps company with tramps becomes their equal."

He returned to his own room and went to bed. He fell asleep thinking about the girl and he woke up thinking about her. And so it continued day after day, month after month until he could barely contain himself. She was present in his life every second of every day.

Finally, he decided to outwit her and put an end to this madness. He went to his mother and said:

"Dear Mother, the time has come for me to get married; find me a bride!"

The king said:

"We must do this in a proper manner and according to protocol. Let us first go to the vizier."

So he asked the vizier:

"Do you have a daughter? We are looking for a bride for my son."

"Yes," said the vizier, "but I have to consult her mother first."

The vizier went to his wife and told her:

"The king wishes to betroth our daughter to his son. What do you say?"

"Tell him, 'Yes!'" said his wife.

"How can I say 'Yes,'" said the vizier, "when she is not yet fully grown?"

"But it's the king's son we're talking about," said his wife. "He cannot be refused! Leave this business to me."

So the vizier's answer to the king was: "Yes! We are honored. You are welcome to our daughter!"

Meanwhile the vizier's wife ran to the vegetable-seller's daughter and said:

"You're our neighbor and we are in trouble. We need you to do us a small favor."

She asked the girl to come to the vizier's house the next day, at the same time that the king's wife was expected, so that the royal party would assume that she was the intended bride.

"I promise you," said the vizier's wife, "that all the gifts they bring for my daughter will be yours. I will give you everything we receive."

"Does that include the jewelry?" asked the girl.

"Including the jewelry!" said the vizier's wife. And the girl agreed.

When the king's wife arrived, the vizier's wife received her with utmost respect and with the hospitality due to such a visitor. For her part, as soon as the king's wife saw the greengrocer's daughter, she was delighted with the young woman, and gave her consent for the betrothal.

The following day, the king's son passed by the vegetable-seller's daughter at her window. After the greeting and chatting and teasing, he announced:

"I am betrothed!"

"So am I!" she answered.

"Truly?" he asked.

"Yes, indeed!" she said.

"Congratulations, then!" he said.

"Congratulations to you too," she responded.

This came as a surprise to the king's son, so he went on to say:

"I'll be married before you!"

"No you won't!" insisted the girl. "I will be the first to get married."

Then the day came for the formal visit by the king and his wife to present the engagement gift to their son's intended bride. The vegetable-seller's daughter was made ready for the occasion. The hairdresser came to arrange her hair and the dressmaker to fit her clothes. She was a beautiful girl to begin with, but on that day her loveliness shone like the moon when it is full. The king and his wife gave her the betrothal gift and returned to their palace. The girl also went home, changed her clothes and sat at her window. The king's son was eager to see her that day. After exchanging the usual banter, he declared:

"Today was my formal engagement."

"Today was my engagement too," said the girl.

"Show me your engagement gift," he challenged.

The girl reached behind the window curtain and brought it out. The young man looked at it and was confused. He kept picking it up and putting it down and thought he was losing his sanity. This was the very jewel he himself had bought. She asked:

"Don't you like it?"

"On the contrary, I like it very much," said the youth, "God grant you happiness and good fortune."

"May God grant you the same," said the girl.

The king's son returned to the palace in silence. He was very troubled. He began to imagine that the vegetable-seller's daughter was haunting him; she was constantly on his mind and he seemed to see her everywhere. He went to his mother with a request that would prove to him that there was no connection between the vizier's daughter, to whom he was betrothed, and the daughter of the grocer next door.

"Mother," he said, "I would like to go for a drive in the carriage with my bride-to-be."

"Let me talk it over with her family," said his mother.

So the king's wife went to the vizier's wife and together they set the time and the place for the encounter. Then, as soon as the king's wife left her, the wife of the vizier rushed to the vegetable-seller's daughter, begging her to accompany the king's son on the outing they had planned. The girl agreed and the prince was ready and waiting for her.

When the young woman entered the carriage she was muffled from head to toe; you could see no part of her. She wore a long coat and a black veil hid her face. In addition, she was wrapped in a black cloak and had a head scarf tightly pinned on one side. The king's son tried to find something that would reveal the girl's identity, but it was impossible. So he started a conversation in order to hear her voice. He said some polite words to her and she responded in kind. The young man was astonished. With his own ears he was hearing the voice of the vegetable-seller's daughter coming from the vizier's daughter's mouth.

"She sounds exactly like the vegetable-seller's daughter," he said to himself. "She is as tall as the vegetable-seller's daughter and as slim. And now it appears she has the same voice! And yet she is the daughter of the vizier. My head is spinning."

During the ride, before he brought her back to the vizier's house, the king's son presented the girl with a beautiful ring.

Once the ride was over, the vegetable-seller's daughter sped home unobserved, changed her clothes and sat at her window as usual. The king's son passed by and said:

"Good evening, O Vegetable-Seller's Daughter."

"Good evening, Prim Princeling, future son-in-law of my father." she replied.

"The sons of sultans do not marry greengrocers' daughters!" he reminded her.

And she repeated:

"He who keeps company with tramps becomes their equal."

The king's son continued:

"Today I took my bride on an outing!"

"Today I went out with my groom," she countered.

"I gave my intended a ring," said the youth.

"And my intended gave me a ring," said the girl.

"Let me see it," he said.

The girl went to fetch the ring. The king's son turned it over and over in his hands then gave it back to her without comment. He could not believe his eyes. This was the very same ring he himself had chosen and bought.

"Don't you like it?" asked the girl.

"On the contrary!" said the youth. "May God grant you happiness and good fortune!"

"God grant you the same!" said the girl.

The king's son returned to the palace thoroughly frustrated. He told his mother that he wanted to get married immediately; he could not wait any longer. So the king's wife went to the wife of the vizier bringing with her the gift of gold that is offered to a bride. Then together they arranged every detail to ensure that the wedding would be a success: from the date of the celebration to the clothes and jewelry to be worn.

That evening the king's son passed by the vegetable-seller's daughter's window and, when they had said their "Good evenings" and teased each other a little, he boasted:

"I have given the bridal gold to my intended."

"My groom has given me my bridal gold too," said the girl.

"Let me see!" said the youth.

She brought out her bridal gold. He examined it then gave it back to her without a word. He could not believe his eyes.

"Is anything wrong?" she asked.

"Not at all," he answered. "God grant you happiness and good fortune!"

"God grant you the same," she said.

The day of the wedding came.

The vegetable-seller's daughter prepared a bridal dais in

her own room before going to the vizier's house. There they dressed her and combed her and decorated her hands and feet with henna dye. They seated her on a dais in their reception room and the Sheikh came to write the marriage contract binding the vizier's daughter to the king's son.

To prepare for the wedding night, the vizier's wife had given the vegetable-seller's daughter her instructions:

"At the close of the celebrations the king's son will go out to thank his parents and his guests and well-wishers. As soon as he leaves, pull out the sack that you will find under the bed in the bridal chamber and place it on top of the bedding. Then turn out the light and go home. There is nothing more I want of you."

"As you wish," said the girl. After all, the vizier's wife had kept her promise and made her and her family rich, so now she had to do her part.

The vizier's wife packed her daughter into a sack and hid her under the bridal bed, telling the child that she should wait until the vegetable-seller's daughter gave the signal for her to take her place on the bed. Meanwhile, the vegetable-seller's daughter went home and sat on her own dais where the king's son could see her.

When they exchanged greetings and challenges as before, the king's son proclaimed:

"Today is my wedding day!"

"It is my wedding day too," said the girl.

"God grant happiness to you both!" said the king's son.

And the girl said:

"May God grant you also and your bride happiness and joy."

That evening, the grocer's daughter in her wedding dress was taken from the vizier's house to the king's palace accompanied by the sound of pipes and drums. The festivities continued and did not stop until the bride retired to the wedding chamber. At last the king's son entered the room. This was the moment to lift the veil that covers the bride's face.

"Glory to her Creator!" he said to himself, "Her beauty rivals a shining star!"

He wanted to talk to her but her loveliness overwhelmed him and he was unable to utter a word. He gestured and pointed to her breasts and face and hands. In time he was able to question her. The vizier's daughter, meanwhile, was hidden under the bed.

"Love of my heart, tell me what is this?" he asked, pointing to her face.

She responded:

"A songbird by the water
To be seen but not sought after."

"And this, what is it?" he asked pointing to her breast.

Her answer was:

"An artist's work a sculpted shape

At this a duped youth may only gape."

"And this and this?" he asked pointing to her henna-patterned hands and feet.

She said:

"Calligraphy and inscription

They open the door for love and affection."

At this point, the king's son excused himself saying that it was his duty to go and thank his family and his guests and friends.

Quickly, the vegetable-seller's daughter pulled out from under the bed the vizier's daughter who was dressed in a wedding gown and jewelry like hers. She placed the girl where she herself had been, blew out the candles and went back to her own home as had been agreed.

When the king's son returned, the bridal chamber was in darkness. He asked:

"Why are the candles out? I am the king's son, a prince! I want the lamps to shine throughout the night until the sun brings morning's light."

There was no reply; the prince guessed that his bride was shy and preferred to stay in the dark. He sat next to her and resumed the play of question and answer as before. He began to ask:

"What is this and this?"

But the child was panicked; she shrieked:

"You should be ashamed! Take away your hands! Don't you know what this is and this? These are my breasts! May God pass judgment on you and on my mother who arranged this marriage!"

The king's son could not believe his ears. He lit the candles and took a look at his bride. He thought his eyes had tricked him; he rubbed them and looked again. What he saw now was very different from what he had seen before. This was a child, as flat as a pane of glass – no bosom, no bottom.

He ran into the garden and fetched a large basket and a rope; he pushed the child into the basket and hung it from the ceiling with the rope. Leaving her there, he hastened to the grocer's house.

The vizier's wife meanwhile had begun to grow anxious about her child. "Gone are the wine jug's fumes; reason now resumes," she quoted to herself. She climbed up to the bridal chamber and knocked on the door whispering her daughter's name, wanting to be reassured that all was well. In a low voice she asked through the closed door,

"Is everything all right, my darling?"

From inside the child shouted:

"O Mother, he has hung me, I have been hung!"

Her mother understood her to say: "He has hugged me! I have been hugged!"

"What an impatient bridegroom," she thought and she asked:

"Do you need anything, my darling?"

"Mother, He has hung me! I have been hung!" repeated the girl.

Every time the mother asked her, the child gave the same answer. One hour passed and then another. Now her mother became worried. She called the servants to break down the door and so she discovered the true condition of her daughter. The rope was cut, the basket lowered, and the child finally rescued.

The people at the palace heard the news. The king and his wife went looking for their son, the bridegroom. The young man, however, had gone to the greengrocer's house and saw through the window the vegetable-seller's daughter seated on her bridal dais.

"Good evening, O Vegetable-Seller's Daughter," he said.

"Good evening, Prim Princeling, future son-in-law of my father!" said the girl.

"Yes, by God, yes!" he exclaimed, "I long to be your father's son-in-law! Will you let me see your face?"

She lifted the veil off her face. Praise the Lord! Was there any woman in the whole world sweeter or more beautiful!

"Love of my heart," said the young man, "What have you been doing to me? Will you marry me now?"

"No," she replied, "I will not marry you until you come with a deputation of petitioners, many and numerous petitioners, to beg and plead with my parents to accept you as my husband."

The next morning the people came, a numerous delegation, to beg and plead with the vegetable seller and his wife to accept the sultan's son as their daughter's husband.

And when the parents were persuaded and agreed...

Hands were shaken
Vows were taken
Judge and lawyer
Wrote the paper
For all to see:
The son of the king and the vegetable-seller's daughter
Bound in marriage, as husband and wife for ever after.

A COW CALLED JOUKHA

ONCE THERE WAS A YOUNG MAN who lived with his mother. He was longing to get married so his mother found a young girl for him. Her name was Baaqa and they were betrothed. After the wedding the young man brought Baaqa home to live with him in his mother's house.

The family owned a cow named Joukha and it became Baaqa's chore every day to milk the cow and take care of her. Then one day, as Baaqa bent down to clear the manure from under the cow, she farted. Horrified by the shame of it, she appealed to the cow:

"God protect you, O Joukha! Will you protect me and promise not to tell?"

The cow was moving her head from side to side to shake off the flies but Baaqa thought the gesture meant that the cow was refusing her and saying, "No!" She ran into the house and came out carrying her wedding gifts which she placed on the ground in front of the cow and begged:

"Please, Joukha! Protect me as God may protect you! Don't tell my husband!"

But Joukha continued to shake her head.

The poor woman returned to the house and brought out her jewelry and put it in front of the cow pleading with her:

"God save you, Joukha! Save me and do not tell my husband!"

And the cow went on shaking her head.

Now Baaqa panicked. She ran to her husband's mother:

"Dear Mother-in-Law," she said, "as I was cleaning under the cow I farted. And Joukha heard me! I have begged and pleaded with her not to tell but she won't listen to me. I offered her my wedding gifts and my jewelry but she has sworn that she will tell my husband!"

"Oh, the disgrace of it!" screamed the woman.

"Oh, the humiliation!" cried the bride.

The mother-in-law was as scared as the bride:

"What shall we say to him?" she asked. "How can we tell him before Joukha speaks and gives me away? What are we to do?"

That was how the young man found his wife and his mother when he came home in the evening.

"Is everything alright, God willing? What is the story? What is the matter with you both?"

His mother answered:

"Dear son," she said, "your wife, Baaqa, is a good woman. She is reasonable. She is loving…"

"Tell me what has happened to her!" he asked. "What is wrong?"

"Nothing, nothing at all," answered his mother.

All the while Baaqa was sobbing and covering her face with both hands.

The young man insisted that he must know what had happened in his absence. So his mother said:

"All right, I'll tell you. But take a seat and try to stay calm."

The young man sat down and his mother told him how his wife was clearing under the cow, how she passed that ill-omened fart and how Joukha refused to protect Baaqa though she pleaded and begged. Then she added:

"You ought to be ashamed, Joukha! After all these years! After all the hay we fed you!"

The young man jumped to his feet in dismay. He could not believe his ears. He addressed the two women saying:

"I shall leave this house, by God! I shall leave the town! I want to see if there is anyone on earth as foolish as the two of you. If I find such a person I'll come right back. Otherwise I will not return."

And off he went.

He walked and walked until he reached the neighboring town. There he saw a woman coming out of her house with an empty sieve in her hands. She stood for a while holding the sieve in front of her then hurried back into the house. After watching her do this twice and three times more, he went up to her and asked:

"O Aunt, what are you doing with your sieve?"

"Dear Son," she said, "my wheat is getting moldy. The flour is mildewed. All the provisions in my house are rotting because the sun never shines in. So with this sieve I carry a little sunshine inside each day."

The young man asked her:

"How much will you pay me if I let the sun shine into your house all day long?"

"I'll give you a hundred liras," she said.

So the man broke into the wall that faced east and broke into the wall that faced west. He built two windows for the woman. Now the sun shone through both openings and filled the house with light and warmth. It dried the wheat and dried the flour and all the provisions in the house! The woman was amazed by the young man's intelligence. She thanked him and paid him the one-hundred liras in cash and coin saying:

"God keep you and grant you a long life!"

The man pocketed the money, took his leave and moved on to another town.

As he walked on his way he came to a streaming wellspring. There he saw a man scooping out water with a tin bucket and emptying it some distance away. The man returned and lowered his bucket again and repeated what he had done before. The water meanwhile was gushing on without a stop. So the young man asked:

"Uncle, what are you trying to do with that bucket?"

He answered:

"I am looking for my wife. She has gone missing! She may have fallen into this wellhead. So I am emptying it of water to see if she fell in here or not."

The young man said:

"If I were to empty the wellhead altogether what will you pay me?"

"I'll give you one-hundred liras," replied the man.

What the young man did was to line up some large rocks in such a way that he diverted the stream. Now the wellhead was empty.

"Take a look, Uncle," he said.

The man looked down carefully but there was no sign of his wife.

"Thank God!" he said, "My wife did not fall into the well, after all. She may have gone home by now. Thank God I met you, young man."

And he paid him the hundred liras, cash and coin, and wished him success:

"God keep you and grant you a long life," he said.

The young man took the money and took his leave then moved on to another town.

He walked and walked until he came to an open space where people were celebrating a wedding. But instead of laughter and music and dancing he heard people keening and weeping and screaming. He edged closer to the crowd and he noticed a man holding a large saw in his hand and people around him pointing to the bridegroom's house. So he asked:

"Why the crying and mourning at a wedding? And what is that large saw for?"

They explained:

"The bride is very tall, so tall that she will not fit in the door. We don't know whether to shorten her by cutting her head or her feet!"

"What will you pay me," he asked, "if I get the bride into the house without touching her or touching the doorway?"

"We will give you one-hundred liras, by God," they said.

This satisfied the young man. He went up to the bride and whispered in her ear:

"Bend your head as you go in the door!"

The bride bent her head and entered the bridegroom's house.

Now the ululations of joy rang out and laughter and music. The dancing began and gladness entered the hearts of all who were present. They gave the young man the hundred liras, cash and coin. They thanked him and thanked the Lord for sending them such a brilliant man. Then they told him:

"If you are single, God grant we celebrate with you on your wedding day! And if you are married, God grant we rejoice with you on the birth of a child!"

The young man took the money and congratulated them

and bid them goodbye. Then his thoughts turned to his wife, Baaqa, and his mother.

"The truth is that there are many far crazier than my wife," he said to himself. "I had better go home now."

And he started walking in the direction of his house.

What about his wife and mother meanwhile? When the neighbor learned that the young man had gone away on his travels, he covered his head with a *kuffieh* cloth held tight with the double black bands of the *iqal*, and disguised himself as a peddler. Then, with a stout staff in one hand, he went out and started shouting:

"I have names for sale! Come buy new names! Names for sale! Who wants to buy a new name?"

The wife heard him and said to her mother-in-law:

"Let me buy a new name, dear Aunt! When my husband returns he will find a new wife waiting for him."

The idea pleased the older woman. She called him:

"O Name-seller, come here!"

The neighbor approached the house and asked the young woman what she was called.

"Baaqa," she said.

"Baaqa? What kind of name is that?" he exclaimed. "It is a name for a cow!"

"No!" said the young woman. "The cow's name is Joukha. And she is the reason I want to change my name."

She asked how much a new name would cost. He said that he would give her a new name and he would accept the cow in exchange, adding:

"This will free you from worrying about her and her stubborn ways."

The young wife was delighted and asked:

"So what name will you sell me?"

"I'll sell you the most beautiful name I have," he said. "You will be called: Fairest-of-Roses-Ornament-of-Houses. Go now and take a bath, comb your hair, put on fresh clothes and rest in a chair without stirring. Then when your husband returns and calls: 'O Baaqa!' Do not utter a word. Talk to him only if he calls you: 'O Fairest-of-Roses-Ornament-of-Houses.'"

The wife and her mother-in-law thanked him and the neighbor took the cow. He kept it in his yard covered with a white sheet.

The young woman bathed and arranged her hair and dressed herself in new clothes. Then she sat quietly waiting for her husband. The man came home. He entered the house and saw his wife sitting inside still as a stone. He called to her:

"O Baaqa!"

She did not respond. So he came closer and said:

"What is troubling you, O Baaqa?"

She did not reply but his mother came in and said happily:

"My dear Son, you have no idea! You don't know what

happened! Your wife has become a new woman. She has bought herself a new name!"

"And what would this new name be, with God's blessing?"

"Her name now is Fairest-of-Roses-Ornament-of-Houses!" said his mother.

So he said:

"O Fairest-of-Roses-Ornament-of-Houses
I have traveled both near and far,
I have met fools as mad as you are."

His wife got up with a smile and greeted him. He asked her how much she had paid for the new name. She told him that she had given the cow, Joukha, in exchange for the name. She added:

"This way we don't have to bother looking after her or dealing with her stubbornness."

The man struck his head with both hands and left the house at a run. This time, he told himself, he would go away and never come back.

Just then he caught sight of his neighbor standing next to a white sheet under which something was moving. When the young man pulled off the sheet, there was the cow, Joukha! He could not stop laughing and the neighbor had to laugh too. Then the young man told his neighbor how he had earned three hundred liras by finding easy answers for simple folk who had foolish problems; how he had brought sunshine into a dark house, diverted a stream from its course, and saved the happiness of a young couple on their wedding day.

The neighbor gave the cow back to its proper owner and received half of the three hundred liras. As for the young husband, he returned to his house pulling Joukha behind him and calling at the top of his voice:

> "O Fairest-of-Roses-Ornament-of-Houses,
> Joukha is coming home on her hooves all four
> To beg your pardon for what she did before."
> *The bird has taken flight*
> *I wish you all good night.*

THE GIRL WHO HAD NO NAME

Long, long ago,
These things happened or maybe no.

THERE WAS A KING, though God alone is Sovereign, who, whenever his wife gave birth to a girl, would have the infant killed. The mother mourned and wept and pleaded with God:

"O Lord, why do you bless me with girl children if they are fated never to stay alive?"

When she next was pregnant and her labor pains began, she called the midwife and said:

"If it is a girl, tell the king that the child was stillborn and keep her safe for me. I'll arrange for a wet nurse and I'll assign women attendants to serve her and care for her."

Her time came and the king's wife gave birth. The baby was a girl. When the king asked about the child, the midwife said:

"It was a stillborn girl."

"God be praised!" said the king. "Her death was through no act of mine: no sin hangs on my neck."

As for the girl, she was hidden in an underground vault and there she was raised till she grew up. She learned to read and write, but had no knowledge of what went on outside the four walls that enclosed her. When she was old enough to understand the tales and novels she read, she realized that there must be a different way of living from her own. The only people she saw were her nurse and the king's wife, who came down to visit her but dared not reveal that she was her mother.

More and more the girl began to wonder about her life. Every day she would ask her nurse some question:

"Dearest Nanny, are we the only people on this earth?"

Her nurse would reply:

"There is no one else."

"Nanny dear," the girl would persist, "in the books there are mothers and fathers and brothers. Don't I have a father or a mother, or brother?"

The nurse would answer:

"I myself am like a mother to you!"

The girl would go on:

"Nanny dear, what is a father like? And a brother, what is he like? There is sky and water in the books. Why don't we have sky and water?"

The nurse's reply always was:

"Have patience, my dear one. You will know everything in good time."

But the girl did not want to wait. She continued to wonder and ask, day after day, insisting that she wanted to understand everything now and not later.

"What things am I supposed to discover? Why should I find out later, why not now?"

The nurse was at a loss, so she said to the girl's mother:

"Dear Mistress, your daughter is growing in height and her questions are growing in number. She will not be patient much longer. What am I to do?"

The mother decided to take the matter into her own hands. She told the nurse that the time had come to admit the truth. So she went down into the vaulted room and sat next to her daughter. She confessed that she was her mother and also told the girl how she had been saved from being killed at birth. When her mother finished speaking, the girl said:

"I cannot bear to stay here any longer!"

Her mother tried to reason with her: she was afraid that the king might kill her if he knew she was still alive. That evening the king's wife called the nurse and said:

"Tomorrow I will be sitting in the garden with the king. Tell my daughter to come to me and say: 'O King's Wife, can you give me an ember to light my fire?' I'll manage things after that."

The nurse ran to tell the girl the good news. She told her that she would be free to go out the next day and instructed her how to act and what to say. The girl was overjoyed and could hardly wait for the next day to dawn. At last the nurse unlocked the door. For the first time the girl was seeing blue sky and green trees and grass. She approached the king and his wife smiling as she gazed at the world around her. When the king saw her his heart melted and he could not turn his eyes away from her. The girl walked up and said:

"O Wife of the King, can you give me an ember to light my fire?"

The king's wife answered impatiently, pretending to be annoyed:

"Did you say an ember? For embers you go to the servants' quarters! Are you asking the king's wife for an ember?"

The girl hung her head and retreated, looking disappointed and embarrassed. That was what her nurse had told her to do. Now the king turned to his wife and asked:

"Who is this girl? Why did you put her off? She has touched my heart. I am sure that there is more to this than an ember to light a fire."

"O King of our Time," pleaded his wife, "Will you grant me the Veil of Immunity!"

"Don't be afraid to tell me who she is," said the king. "You will not be harmed."

So the king's wife explained:

"You need to know the truth so I have to tell you that this girl is your very own child. They lied to you when they said she was stillborn. Here she is, alive and well – our daughter!"

Now the king broke in and asked for the girl to be called back at once.

So the king's wife called her and the girl came, a questioning look on her face about all that was happening.

The king asked her:

"What is your name?"

"I don't know," said the girl.

The king invited her to go up into the palace, saying:

"Take a look at yourself in the mirror. Try on the dresses that are laid out there. Put them on one after the other and do this until you decide on a name that suits you. Then come back and let me know what you want to be called."

Up went the girl, accompanied by her mother, whose heart was filled with joy. She was left to choose a gown and a name that pleased her. Standing in front of the mirror, she put on one dress and took off the next and saw that she was beautiful. When she finally made her decision she went down to the king and said:

"I have chosen. My name shall be Lady Grace, Sitt Rafeeah!"

"Then welcome to Sitt Rafeeah," said the king and clasped her to his breast. He acknowledged that he was her father and that his wife was her mother. He thanked the nurse and the midwife. Then he ordered a celebration to announce to the people that he had a daughter. He called her "my Sitt Rafeeah." Now young men from every part, princes and sons of kings, raced to ask for her hand in marriage. When the girl made her choice she picked a prince whose beauty shone like the light of the moon.

The king had gratified his daughter at every turn and provided for all her needs, as they say, "lifting her with indulgence and setting her down in comfort." However, a girl has to get married and go to her husband. Sitt Rafeeah was formally promised to the handsome prince and became his bride.

Her father and his were both agreed.

The judge was summoned with all speed.

The contract was written and read.

The happy news was widely spread.

Now the prince, the bridegroom, had seven first cousins, young girls who had waited long for him to choose his bride from among themselves, as was the custom and tradition. But this he did not do. Instead, he had chosen a stranger he had not even seen. The cousins were furious. They crowded round the prince whispering to each other but loud enough for him to hear.

"Our cousin is a handsome youth," said one. "Why did he have to choose a squint-eyed bride?"

"She not only squints but is blind in one eye," said another.

The rest followed suit, each one citing some failing in the bride:

"I heard that she is lame."

"They say that she is simple-minded."

"Yes, she is a simpleton and also rude!"

"It is enough that she is so full of herself."

"She has all of the seven deadly vices!"

After hearing this, the prince thought:

"Now I see why her father waited so long before announcing that he has a marriageable daughter whom he calls Sitt Rafeeah! I am sure my cousins know what they are talking about." Boiling with rage, he departed from the wedding feast and fled.

The celebrations came to an end. The bride remained alone. All night long she sat on the dais in her wedding gown waiting for her bridegroom but he did not come. The well-wishers went home; the lights were dimmed and still the bridegroom did not appear. Finally the girl asked the prince's mother why he had not come.

"Dear Mother-in-Law," she said, "why has my husband not come?"

The woman explained that her son had left after hearing his cousins whispering. She had tried to persuade him to see his bride for himself before believing what they said. It was no use.

"It is up to you to sort this out, my child," she sighed.

The girl said nothing. She was thinking out a plan.

In the morning she asked her mother-in-law the whereabouts of the prince's quarters. The mother said that he lived in the wing of the palace that overlooked the gardens.

On the following day, Sitt Rafeeah put on a pink dress with pink slippers to match and went down into the garden to look for a rosebud to place in her hair. She made her way through the garden breaking every flower and plant and shrub in her path until she found a rosebush. She picked a pink rosebud, fastened it in her hair and returned to her room. Towards evening the king's son went into the garden and saw the broken flowers lying on the ground. He was puzzled but said nothing.

The next day, Sitt Rafeeah wore a violet-colored dress and slippers to match and went into the garden to look for violets to pin onto her dress. She broke every flower and plant and shrub in her path until she came upon some violets that she picked and pinned onto her dress. At sunset, the king's son went into the garden and again he saw destruction all around. This time he was angry and he decided to keep watch in the garden to see whose work this was.

On the third day, Sitt Rafeeah went down into the garden in a white dress with matching white slippers. The king's son soon found her but he did not know who she was because he had not yet seen his bride's face. Her beauty all but blinded him. He walked up to greet her. His heart warmed to her charm; his anger dissolved. The girl, on the other hand, was well aware that this was her betrothed and the husband who had disappeared at her wedding, but she acted as if she did not know him. The king's son asked her who she was and what she was doing.

"I stroll around this garden and talk to the flowers," she said. "Can you really talk to the flowers?" he asked. Then, pointing to a violet at his feet, he said, "Look at this one – what is it saying?"

She replied:

"The flower is saying:

I am the Violet, the sultan of garden and field,

Lowly my stem, but sweet my scent; to me all yield.

I leave for a year,

Twelve months I disappear

Yet on my return

All hearts still burn

With love, as before."

The king's son had no idea what the girl meant by this but he continued to stare at her in rapture. They passed by a jasmine bush and the girl addressed it:

"O Jasmine, Jasmine, trained to grow against our wall,

Love me and I vow not to let you break or fall.

You are my Mecca wherever you may stray,

Your name is on my lips every time I pray.

Alas, my arm is short and you beyond my reach."

The young man still did not understand what she was hinting at. They walked side by side until they came to a leafy arbor by a pool. She said:

"O climbing vine,

Does love not pine

When forced to part

From his sweetheart?"

Looking at the king's son, the girl repeated the question:

"Would not a lover weep

For a love he cannot keep?"

Not grasping what she was trying to say the young man was confused and answered:

"Yes, yes, he must surely weep!"

The girl sat at the edge of the pool and pulled a handkerchief from her pocket to wipe the tears that wet her cheeks. The king's son meanwhile noticed nothing. The girl said:

"O pool of clear and shining water
Is not love's loss the heart's disaster?"

"Do you talk to things as well as flowers?" asked the youth.

In reply the girl pointed to a lamp hanging from a tree, and addressed it tearfully:

"Call me tyrant! Why else assault
A lamp that knows no sin and has no fault!
My lamp hangs from a golden chain
It burns with a brave and lively flame
Yet I pray to God up in the sky
To snuff it out and let it die.
Why and for what reason?
He trusts his lying cousins
He will not seek the truth!"

The king's son listened to her overcome with love and adoration but without any notion that he was the subject of her verses. At first the girl had been annoyed but now she was sad. She decided to return to her room. As she climbed the wooden stair she tripped. The king's son seized her hand to stop her fall. He saw that she had cut her ankle and quickly tore his sash to make a bandage for her foot. The girl said:

"My heart was breaking
My knees were shaking
I fell upon the stair
And saw Death waiting there.
Give me pen, give me paper
With black ink to write a letter
To the one who abandoned me and fled."

The girl went to her mother-in-law and asked to be the one to bring the prince his dinner without revealing who she was. The king's wife consented. When it was time for the evening meal the prince sat at table sunk in thought. He knew that he loved the girl in the garden and wished to marry her but he was married already to a woman he had never seen. He asked for a glass of water. The girl brought it to him. When he did not lift his head, she dropped the tray so the glass shattered on the floor. Still the prince did not turn his head. The girl went for another glass and the same thing happened. The third time the prince lost his temper and raised his voice:

"Why are you so clumsy-footed?"

"And who was it who tore his sash and tied this clumsy foot?" she asked.

The king's son shook himself and stood up. He looked the girl fully in the face. He heard his mother say:

"This is your bride, my son. This is none other than Sitt Rafeeah!"

He rushed to take her in his arms. Then the wedding was celebrated anew. For seven days and nights all food and drink was from the king's purse.

So they were married and very glad
May such joy for everyone be had.
Say: "Amen."

THE FROG AND HIS WIFE

There was a man who had a woolen cloak
He trimmed it here
He trimmed it there
He turned it downside up and inside out…
But let me tell the story from the beginning:

THERE WAS A FROG AND HIS WIFE who lived happily with each other. They quarreled and they made peace. They were sad and they were glad. Then one day, as they were sunning themselves they fell asleep. But all at once the frog's wife dived into the water nearby. Splash! She wet the frog and soaked him through and through. He leapt up with a start and yelled:

"What a silly thing to do,
For someone old as you!
An outrage
At your age!"

The frog's wife was stunned. She was speechless with anger. The words stuck in her throat and she could not make a sound in reply. Instead she turned around and left. Back to her parents' house she went.

The frog stayed behind frustrated, hurt, and depressed. He no longer sunned himself nor did he swim but sat on a stone, lonesome and alone.

The donkey walked by and asked him why he was sad:

"Hey! What is plaguing you, our Uncle the Doctor, why are you looking so distressed?"

The frog replied:

"Your Uncle the Doctor is in a hole!

His wife, sweetest of souls,

Has packed and gone.

So now he is on his own."

The donkey asked:

"Do you want me to try

And bring her back, by and by?"

"By God, it would be a big favor!" said the frog.

The donkey went to the frog's wife and knocked on her door.

Without opening, she asked:

"Who knocks at a private person's door,

With no invitation sent out before?"

The donkey replied:

"I am your Uncle the Donkey,

Also known as Ass,

Professor of All-and-Sundry,

Preeminent in my class."

She unlocked the door and demanded:

"What do you want?"

"I want you to accompany me to our Uncle the Doctor," he said with a smile.

"That I won't!" she snapped and banged the door shut.

The donkey went back to the frog and reported that his mission had met with failure:

"She said she will not come."

So the frog sat on his stone, lonesome and alone.

The camel walked by and asked him why he was sad:

"Hey! Our Uncle, the Doctor! Why so down in the mouth?"

The frog said:

"Your Uncle the Doctor is in a hole!

His wife, sweetest of souls,

Has packed and gone

So now he is on his own."

The camel said:

"Do you want me to try

And bring her back, by and by?"

"Our Uncle the Donkey has already gone to her, but she does not want to come," explained the frog.

"Maybe I can persuade her and she'll agree to come with me," said the camel.

"It would be a great favor, by God!" said the frog.

The camel went to the frog's wife and knocked at her door. From inside she asked:

"Who knocks at a private person's door

With no invitation sent before?"

The camel said:

"I am your Uncle the Camel,

Also known as Dromedary,

Across dry deserts I travel

Heavy the loads that I carry."

She pushed open the door and inquired:

"What is it you want?"

"I want you to come with me to our Uncle the Doctor," said the camel with his wide grin.

"No. I won't!" she exclaimed and locked the door.

The camel went back to the frog and told him that his attempt had failed:

"She said she will not come."

So the frog sat on his stone, lonesome and alone.

The horse went by and asked him why he was sad:

"Hey! What's up, our Uncle the Doctor? Are you in mourning?"

The frog said:

"Your Uncle the Doctor is in a hole!

His wife, sweetest of souls,

Has packed and gone

So now he is on his own!"

The horse said:

"Do you want me to try

And bring her back by and by?"

"Others have tried before you," answered the frog. "Our Uncle the Donkey has gone to her already and she refused. Then our Uncle the Camel went and she still won't come."

"Let me intercede! With me she will surely come," said the horse.

"By God," said the frog, "That would be a grand favor!"

So the horse went to the frog's wife and knocked on the door.

Through the wall the frog's wife asked:

"Who knocks at a private person's door,

With no invitation sent out before?"

The horse replied:

"I am your Uncle the Horse,

Also known as Stallion,

I race the longest course;

My rider is the Sultan!"

The frog's wife was smiling as she flung open her door. She asked:

"What can I do for you?"

"Come with me. We are going to our Uncle the Doctor," the horse commanded.

"Of course I'll come. It is an honor to ride the horse that carries our Sultan," she said. "How can I refuse?"

And with one long leap she landed on his back. The horse took her right to her husband, the Doctor. As soon as the frog caught sight of her, he began to jump for joy, skipping around her and loudly singing:

"Spread and put on display

Bright silks in colors gay

Hide and pack away
All that's black or gray
The prince's heart in pain was churning
O Joy! His princess is now returning!"
The frog's wife, however, stayed on the horse's back.
"Come down," said the frog, "dismount!"
"No!" said his wife.
"What are you waiting for?" asked the frog.
The frog's wife stood on the horse's back looking down at her husband and said:
"I will not move until I have listed all your failings. Answer me: Why is your head so swollen?"
"I wear a cashmere turban!"
"Why are your eyes so bloodshot?"
"In the officers' club, I drink a lot."
"Why are your legs so long and thin?"
"They fit my soldier's boots of stout goatskin."
The frog's wife took a long look at her husband. She decided that he was a model of virility, after all. So she jumped into his lap. And from then on the frog and his wife sunned themselves and lived happily with each other again…

Until this day
They jump and play
They eat and drink and sleep and snore
Content, they ask for nothing more.

JUBAYNA THE FAIR

There was or maybe no
It was a long time ago…

THERE WAS A WOMAN who was childless. She had never tasted the joy of carrying or giving birth to an infant. One day, as she was making ewe's milk cheese, she held up a piece and begged the Lord to grant her a daughter as white and as tender as the cheese in her hand. She would call the child Jubayna, diminutive of the word for cheese.

God heard her prayer. She became pregnant and gave birth to a beautiful girl as fair and as fine as the freshest cheese. She called her Jubayna and raised her with love and care.

The child in a story grows fast. Soon Jubayna was a young woman. The other girls in the village envied her and resented the way she was pampered and indulged. One day, when they were going to pick wild apples, they invited her to join them:

"Come with us, Jubayna, we are planning to go out for crab apples."

Jubayna asked for permission from her mother. The woman was hesitant but eventually she agreed:

"Take good care of her! She is my only child."

So Jubayna went with the other girls. When they reached the place, the girls asked Jubayna to climb into the tree and shake the crab apples down. They said:

"Climb up and we'll fill your bucket for you."

Jubayna clambered into the tree and shook its branches. The ripe fruit rained down covering the ground. The girls filled the buckets choosing the good apples for themselves and the gnarled ones for Jubayna's bucket. They had put pebbles in it first.

On the way home the girls stopped and said:

"Let's empty our buckets and see who has the best fruit."

When Jubayna saw the stones in the bottom of her bucket, her eyes filled with tears and when she noticed that all her crab apples were spoiled, she stood up, took her bucket and said that she was going back to fill it with the most beautiful fruit of all. She would choose her apples one by one. She retraced her steps and reached the tree just as the sun was about to set.

There was an old man standing there. He asked:

"What are you doing here, Jubayna, all by yourself?"

"I'm picking crab apples!"

Jubayna did not know that this old man was a spirit in human shape! She recounted to him how she had been tricked by her friends and that now she wanted to pick the best crab apples for herself.

"If you do as I say," said the old man, "I will fill your bucket with the largest and most attractive fruit on the tree. Then I will blow one breath and you will find yourself back with your mother before your friends get home."

She asked:

"But what do you want me to do in return?"

He said:

"All I want is for you to come to me whenever I burn one of the hairs of my head, and let me suck the end of your finger."

Jubayna accepted. So the old man filled her bucket with the best of the crab apples, then he sucked the end of her finger and blew her home to her mother. After that, whenever he burnt one of his hairs at sunset, Jubayna went to him and he sucked her fingertip. This continued until Jubayna began to grow thin and weak. Then one day she decided she would not do this any longer and she ran away. She ran and ran with the old man running after her shouting:

"I'll change myself into a tom cat and catch you!"

"It is unlucky for me to go near cats," replied Jubayna.

"I'll change into a horse!" he yelled.

"It is not proper for me to ride horses," she said and went on running.

"I'll change into a camel!" he said. But by then Jubayna had run a long way and did not hear this last threat. She went home and was able, for a time, to live in peace.

When the season for the Hajj, the pilgrimage to Mecca, came round, everyone went to the cattle market to choose a suitable camel for the journey. Jubayna picked a camel with colorful tassels, and bells decorating its neck. Then, with the setting of the sun, the caravan set off for Mecca.

At the first stopping place everyone dismounted except Jubayna. She was unable to move and no one could pull her off her camel; it was as if she had been glued to it. They left the problem for the morning, citing the proverb, "An early start in the mornings brings success and big earnings." And they all went to sleep. Jubayna was forced to stay where she was on the back of her camel. But before sunrise, when it was still dark, the camel transformed itself into a ghoul. Jubayna realized that this was the old man who had hounded her. He said:

"I don't have the heart to kill you and I don't have the heart to devour you but I cannot leave you alone. I will blow on you and turn you into a mangy dog. People will be disgusted by you and no one will touch you. And I warn you, should you take off your dog skin, even if only for a single day, you will die."

Then he blew a single breath, which transformed Jubayna into a mangy dog, and disappeared. As it happened, the ghoul died soon afterwards, but Jubayna had no knowledge of that.

In the morning there was no trace of Jubayna or her camel among the pilgrims' convoy. Instead there was a mangy dog that kept following in the caravan's wake. Everyone would give it a kick or shoo it away for fear of the mange spreading.

When they reached the city, Jubayna left the pilgrims and ran through the streets until she happened upon a house belonging to an old woman. The woman saw that the dog was hungry and tossed some food for it on the ground. But the dog did not move towards it. When the woman placed the food in a dish the dog was willing to eat. And so Jubayna stayed in the house eating the old woman's food and sleeping on a straw mat on her floor.

Every day, in the early morning, Jubayna would make her way to the Sultan's gardens, which were planted with every kind of fruit tree. There she would chant these words:

"O keeper of the prince's seal
Seal the eyes of the watchman here
So I can pick some fruit and fill my basket
For a kind old lady – else I would not ask it."

While the eyes of the watchman were firmly shut and he could not see her, Jubayna would shed her dog skin and bathe in the garden pool and swim about. But she always put on her dog skin again before returning to the old woman's house. The people in the palace were puzzled by the disappearance of the fruit from the garden. So the sultan's son decided to keep watch. When he saw Jubayna in the water taking her swim, he was struck with her beauty and her fair complexion and instantly felt that he loved her. Keeping her in sight, he followed at a distance without her noticing and discovered where she lived. Then he hurried home to the palace calling to his mother:

"O Mother, dear Mother,

Put away all signs of gladness
Spread out the colors of sadness
Your son has a grievous illness
That no drug or doctor can cure."

His mother said:

"May God keep you whole, dear son. What is the matter with you? What do you want?"

"I want to get married," he said.

"What blessed news!" said his mother, "A thousand blessings on you, dear Son! You can choose any girl you want. Which of your cousins do you wish for? Is it your uncle's daughter? Is it your aunt's daughter?"

"I want the mangy dog that lives with the old woman in the alley," he said.

Striking one hand against the other, his mother cried:

"Did you say mangy dog? Impossible! My son, the son of a Sultan, wanting to marry a mangy dog!"

She tried to dissuade the young man but it was no good. Reluctantly, she went to the old woman to ask about the dog.

"It will only eat off a plate," said the old woman, "and it will only sleep on this mat."

In the end, the Sultan's wife accepted the dog for her son. The marriage took place quietly in secret and no announcements were made.

When the young couple was alone in their room, the prince asked Jubayna to take off her dog skin. She barked in refusal. He threatened and she barked again. Then he told her how he had seen her bathing in the garden pool and how he had loved her in that first instant and how, if she was afraid of anything, he would protect her. He said:

"Remember that you are my wife now and I am your husband. You have to trust me!"

Jubayna stepped out of the dog skin. And there she stood:

A young woman of pleasing grace

Radiant as the sun at noon

Who could rightly tell the moon:

"You may set, for I can shine in your place."

Her husband seized the dog skin, wanting to get rid of it, but she managed to hold on to a small piece. He handed the skin to the keeper of the bathhouse fires and told him to burn it. Jubayna meanwhile rubbed her brow with the piece she had, and it made her even more beautiful than she already was.

Next morning, Jubayna guessed that the supernatural spirit who had menaced her must have died. She had spent a whole day and night without the dog skin, and nothing harmful had happened to her. So she felt free to tell her husband her whole story.

Now the prince was ready to celebrate his wedding. He invited Jubayna's people to attend. His own parents came, and his brothers also. They ridiculed him, mocking and jeering and asking to meet his dog wife. He said:

"First you must give me your wedding gifts for the bride."

After every member of his family had offered him the traditional gift of bridal gold, he said:

"Come, Jubayna!"

The young woman entered. Her beauty shone like a candle in the dark. God's name be upon her! What a breathtaking sight!

Everyone was delighted. Everyone ululated with joy. The bridegroom said:

"Mother, let the wedding feast be carried to the terrace on the roof."

He built a wooden ladder into which he hammered nails so that as his bride climbed up each rung her scarf would catch on a nail and slip off. Then all the people of the town would see Jubayna without her head veil and know that the prince had married not a mangy dog but a woman of astonishing beauty.

The town crier was sent to announce:

"For seven days and seven nights no one shall eat or drink except from the prince's palace."

Jubayna's parents came. The wedding banquet was carried to the roof. The bride was radiant and, as she climbed the ladder up to the terrace, at each rung her head veil caught on a nail and fell, while the prince stood by to hand her another in its stead.

> *They went on to live together in happiness and glory*
> *May God sweeten the days of all who enjoy this story.*

BALDHEAD IN THE GARDEN

There was or perhaps there was not,
It may have happened or maybe not,
In this story we say a lot;
The truth hangs from the tongue of the narrator
As a grape hangs from the vine in the arbor.

THERE WAS A WOMAN who lived with her husband and their two children. With them also was the orphaned son of the husband's first wife. The father loved his motherless child and favored him above the stepmother's two sons. The orphaned boy owned a young horse, a filly that he had raised and cared for since childhood. This horse was on constant alert to warn the boy about his stepmother.

One day the woman called all three children and told them that she had stewed two stuffed geese for Eid, the holiday. Her stepson was to have one whole goose for himself.

"No," said the boy, "let me have an equal share with my brothers."

"You are the eldest and most deserving," said the woman. "I want you to have a whole goose; I have stuffed it with rice and spice and pistachio nuts."

The boy dished out a portion of the food and ran to feed his horse. The filly took one sniff at the dish and refused to eat.

"It is poisoned," she told him. "Your goose is stuffed with poison!"

The boy returned to his brothers and in passing, spun the serving tray so that the poisoned goose lay before the woman's two sons and the other goose in front of himself.

No sooner had the two sons taken a couple of bites than they fell down dead. The woman realized what had happened and decided to rid herself of the orphan's horse.

Some days later, she rubbed her face with saffron water to stain it yellow and laid some toasted bread under her sheet. Then she took to her bed turning this way and that so that the crisped bread crackled with every move.

"Oh, oh, my poor bones!" she loudly groaned. "Oh, oh, I can hear them breaking!"

"God keep you and grant you good health, O Wife of my Father," said the boy. "What is the matter with you? What do you need to make you feel better?"

That day the filly had said to the youth:

"Up till now you have been the one your stepmother tries to harm. But watch, today she is determined to harm me!"

When the stepmother answered the boy she said:

"The doctor told me that the only cure is for me to eat the heart of a young female horse with white markings on three of her legs."

"A filly with three white feet?" exclaimed the boy. "The only horse that fits that description is my own dear filly! I raised her and trained her myself; let me take one more ride on her and say goodbye."

"O dearest boy! Your stepmother's darling!" said the woman. "There is no need for farewells! Keep your filly! What does it matter if I never recover?"

"Oh no, Stepmother, you will surely recover!" said the boy. He saddled the filly, rode up and down shouting "Goodbye!" not once or twice but three times then waved to his father's wife and galloped off.

He continued on horseback until he came to a fork in the road. There he dismounted and pulled two hairs from the filly's mane. He told her that he would burn one of the hairs to summon her if ever he was in trouble.

"Now go!" He said, "May safety be your companion!"

The filly trotted off in one direction and the youth took the other. Continuing on foot he arrived at an imposing castle, standing by itself, far from any sign of human life. He could smell meat being grilled and it made him hungry. He went closer to take a look. He saw a ghoul cutting up lamb's meat, groping to count the pieces: "1, 2, 3, 4, 5, 6, 7!" Just then, the ghoul had a sneezing fit. So the boy crept up quietly and stole a piece of the meat, then hid out of the way to eat it. The ghoul counted his meat again: "1, 2, 3, 4, 5, 6…" When he felt for the seventh piece and found it missing, he was furious. Sniffing right and left he growled:

"I smell a human smell! If there is anyone present here, let him answer now, or I will eat him for my dinner. If he answers, I will not touch him."

Hearing this, the young man came out of his hiding place and jumped in front of the ghoul and said:

"I am here, Father!"

"Are you really my son?" asked the ghoul.

"Of course I am!" said the boy.

So the ghoul said:

"If you truly are a child of mine, you will be strong like me. As a test, I shall piss on you. If I carve a hole in your middle, I will devour you. But if your stomach remains untouched, I'll know you are my son."

The ghoul had been blinded by his sister and he could not see a thing. So the boy held a stone slab across his middle and lay down on his back. As the ghoul stood over him, the boy said:

"Go on, Father! Let fly!"

The boy had to hold the slab with both his hands. The ghoul's flow was so powerful it pierced the stone! Throwing the slab aside, the boy stood up and leaned forward so the ghoul could feel his stomach.

"Yes, you are indeed my son," said the ghoul. And he enveloped the youth in his cloak.

Now it was the ghoul's daily task to drive his flock, his sheep and his goats, out to pasture, going wherever there was grass. But the herd had grazed till the ground was bare.

"Let me help you, Father," said the boy, "I'll pasture your flock for you."

"Just keep out of my sister's way," warned the ghoul. "She's the one who blinded me."

The boy set out with the ghoul's sheep and goats and found that the pasture nearby was dry and barren. Towards the sister's place, however, a spread of green grass covered the ground. So the boy led the flock to crop in that direction, while he sat under a tree singing to himself a shepherd's song. Suddenly, he saw dust rising in the distance and the ghoul's sister with a mass of tangled hair approaching as fast as her legs could carry her, roaring at the top of her voice. He quickly climbed up the tree and stood on the highest branch. The ghoul's sister stopped below and called up to him:

"Come, my love, my own brother's son! Climb down, dear nephew!"

"Why don't you climb up to me?" asked the boy.

"How do you expect me to clamber up the tree?" she asked.

"Let me get hold of your hair and pull you up," said the boy.

So he caught hold of the sister's hair but he wrapped it tightly round one of the branches.

"Give me the medicine, Aunt, to cure my father," he said.

"What medicine and what cure are you talking about?" asked the ghoul's sister.

"O Aunt," said the boy, "you were the one who blinded

your brother and now you must give me the medicine to cure him. Let me have it or else I'll leave you in this tree hanging by your hair."

The ghoul's sister told him where to find a jar of ointment. He rubbed it on the eyes of one of the sheep. The sheep went blind, unable to see. So the boy rushed back to the ghoul's sister:

"O Aunt," he cried. "First you blinded your brother and now you have blinded his sheep. Give me the right medicine or I will leave you hanging here so the wild dogs can come and tear you to pieces."

She told him where the medicine was. He rubbed it on the sheep's eyes and the sheep regained its sight. Then he cut off the ghoul's sister's head and returned to the ghoul with the healing ointment and the flock of sheep and goats.

"Father," he said, "I have come to cure your blindness and give you back your sight."

"What are you saying, son," said the ghoul. "I am no match for my sister. I have never been able to face her myself so how could you?"

"I have killed her," said the boy, "and here is her head. I have brought you the medicine that will cure you."

He placed the sister's head on the ghoul's knee and rubbed first one eye and then the other with the ointment. The ghoul stood up and opened his eyes.

"Dear boy!" he said, "Let me look at you. I can see you now and see my home and the sheep and the goats! Ask me for anything you desire and you shall have it."

The ghoul gave the boy the keys to his castle. But first he cautioned him that there were two keys he must never use; they unlocked two rooms he must never enter.

For a time, the orphan boy lived in the ghoul's castle happy and contented. Then, one day, he could not resist the urge to open the forbidden rooms. He opened the door to the first room and found that it contained a stream of liquid silver. When he dipped his hands into the stream, all ten fingers turned to silver. He opened the second room and saw a stream of liquid gold. He leaned down to take a better look and a lock of his hair brushed against the stream so all his hair turned to gold! The boy quickly locked up the two rooms and covered his hands and hair so the ghoul would not guess what had happened. But the ghoul had seen him and knew that he had disobeyed his orders. So the youth was forced to confess.

"I went against your wishes, Father," he said, "I went into the forbidden rooms."

"This means you cannot stay here any longer," said the ghoul, "You must continue on your travels and fend for yourself from now on."

Before bidding the ghoul farewell, the boy slaughtered one of the sheep, took out the stomach, cleaned it and turned it into a leather cap. He wore the cap to hide his gold hair but it made him look like a bald man. Then, taking leave of the ghoul, he went on his way.

He walked and walked until he arrived at a king's palace where preparations were being made for some important event. This king had three daughters for whom he wanted to find suitable husbands. It was the custom in that city for suitors to pass below the window of a marriageable girl so that she could throw an apple to the one she chose to be her husband.

At the palace, the orphaned youth asked if there was any work he could do. They gave him a job as gardener and a nickname; they called him "Baldhead-in-the-Garden." So the boy began to work in the palace grounds. He cared for the plants during the day and at sunset he took off his leather cap and rested. Now it happened that one night the king's youngest daughter was looking out of her window and saw the youth's golden hair gleaming in the moonlight. In that moment, she decided that when she threw her apple, it would be to this young man.

On the day of the big celebration, the king's three daughters stood at their window while, one by one, the young men of the kingdom walked past below. Each girl made her choice and the youngest daughter tossed her apple to Baldhead-in-the-Garden. Her father was not pleased.

"You are creating an embarrassment for me!" he said to her, "How can I accept someone like this Baldhead-in-the-Garden as my son-in-law?"

"If I don't marry him, I will not marry at all," she declared.

"Go, then! Go live like him and share his poverty," retorted her father.

"I will gladly share his life, whatever it may be," she said.

The three sisters were married, the weddings were celebrated and the youngest daughter departed with Baldhead-in-the-Garden.

"I saw you from my window," she said, "I saw your golden hair. I don't believe that you are a gardener!"

"Baldhead-in-the-Garden is what I am!" he replied.

She gave him fine clothing but he refused to wear it. At night he slept on the doorstep of the house. "My time has not come yet," he explained.

Then one day the king fell ill. He summoned the husbands of his two older daughters and asked them to bring him lion's milk for a cure. The youngest daughter heard this and ran to tell her husband.

The youth set light to one of his filly's hairs. In an instant she stood before him. He put on the fine clothing, mounted the horse and rode away to distant parts where he found the lion's milk. On the way home he met his two brothers-in-law setting out on their quest. They didn't recognize him, and as they chatted by the roadside, they told him where they were going and for what purpose.

"I have some lion's milk with me," said the youth, "but it is costly."

"We will gladly pay whatever you ask for and more," they cried, "Just name your price."

He told them that what he wanted was for the two of them to hand over their rings. He pocketed the two rings and gave the men the lion's milk. Then he returned to his wife.

Time passed. War broke out between the king and a neighboring kingdom. The king marched out to battle at the head of his army with his two sons-in-law at his side. He did not ask for any help from the husband of his youngest daughter. The army was on the point of defeat; it began to retreat. In a panic, Baldhead-in-the-Garden's wife begged her husband to save the king her father.

So Baldhead set light to the second hair from his filly's mane, and as soon as the horse appeared, he rode out in his fine suit, swinging his sword and killing the king's enemies. He fought so bravely that the king was able to declare victory. During the battle, Baldhead-in-the-Garden was wounded and the king offered him his royal sash to tie his arm.

The battle was over and the youth returned to his wife. He was exhausted and threw himself on his bed just as he was while his wife sat beside him. He showed her the bandage on his arm that was her father's sash and the two rings that had belonged to her brothers-in-law. While the young woman was still caring for her tired husband and making him comfortable, the king burst into the house rebuking her in anger:

"Every able-bodied man in the kingdom came to fight alongside us," he said. "Everyone, that is, except for this lazy Baldhead, your husband. It was a brave stranger, an unknown hero, who saved us in the end!"

The girl stood up to face her father and the king saw his own sash in her hand and the seal rings of his two sons-in-law. He kissed his daughter and her husband. Gazing at Baldhead-in-the-Garden with admiration and respect, the king begged to be forgiven for the past.

The young couple celebrated their wedding anew
They enjoyed peace and prosperity their whole life through
Until the time came for them to pay Death his due.

KING SOLOMON AND
THE QUEEN OF BIRDS

It may or may not be so,
For it happened long ago.
In the days before men used coins and minted gold,
When goods were bartered, not bought and sold,
King Solomon, peace be upon his soul,
Ruled with justice and clemency, we have been told…

EVERY FRIDAY, THE KING OPENED wide his palace gates and received all those who wished to see him. The people came: this one to report his news, that one to explain his views; one man to seek counsel, another to complain; some praising and thankful, others ready to blame….

In those days King Solomon conversed with all living creatures and addressed the animals in their own tongue.

One morning, a chiffchaff bird saw her reflection in the water of a lake and she said to herself:

"How beautiful I am! It is true I am very, very small. But I wear a golden collar round my neck and my robe is olive green and walnut brown. Delicate and straight is my beak and my posture most refined. Surely I am entitled to be queen of all the birds."

So on one of those Fridays when the palace gates were opened, the little bird entered along with the other visitors.

King Solomon, peace be upon him, received her and she approached and said:

"O Messenger of God, behold: I am very, very small but I wear a golden collar around my neck and my robe is olive green and walnut brown. My beak is delicate and straight and my posture most refined. Surely I am entitled to be the queen of birds! Crown me, O King Solomon, make me queen of all the birds!"

King Solomon replied:

"We shall look into the matter."

She came back the following Friday and pleaded and begged:

"Let it please you, O King Solomon, to crown me queen of the birds!"

"All in good time," he said.

She returned a third time, determined and persistent, saying:

"I beseech and implore you, O King Solomon, crown me queen of the birds."

But he shook his head and said nothing.

After that the little bird went back to the palace and stood before the king threatening him and shouting at the top of her voice:

"O Solomon, our King and Sovereign

Unless you make me queen of the birds and give me the crown

I will roll in the dust of your protected grounds

I will rub the dirt into everything you own
And what is now a palace will be your ruined home."
The king nodded and said:
"Little bird, I consent.
But first go find me a wooden stick
That is neither thin nor thick
A stick that is not green or dry or short or long
And as soon as you are done,
I will crown you queen of all the birds."
So off the little bird went, flying and flying! She fluttered from tree to tree, hopping from this twig to that, turning her head right and left as she looked and looked for that wooden stick. But every time she found a piece of wood she rejected it crying:

"Tsk! Tsk! No! No! It's too long! Tsk! Tsk! It's too short! No, too thick! No, too thin!"

The little bird has not stopped looking to this day. She hops and flutters and turns her head to right and left searching with her interrupted chirp of: "Tsk! Tsk! No! No! Tsk! Tsk! No! No!"

You can see her for yourself hopping about looking right and left. Because of her Tsk! here and Tsk! there, people sometimes call her the "Tsk-Tsker." And her real name, Chiffchaff, also sounds like her chirping.

The chiffchaff is still looking for the wooden stick.
That is neither thin nor thick
A stick not green, not dry
Not short, not long
To give King Solomon
So he may crown her queen of birds by and by.

SITT YADAB

LONG AGO, IN A FORMER TIME and another clime, there was a young girl named Yadab. She lived in the city with her father and mother who loved her dearly. They indulged her every wish and refused her nothing. Lady Yadab, Sitt Yadab, is what they liked to call her. When she needed shoes they ordered clogs to be made for her: one shoe of silver and one of gold. The girl was an only child. Her parents had not been blessed with a boy. Her father sent Sitt Yadab to the kuttab, the Koran school, just as he would have sent a son, to learn to read and write.

So every morning Sitt Yadab left the house and walked to school. One day, the Sheikh who taught them told the students to come early, with the dawn, and whoever arrived first would receive a prize.

Sitt Yadab was a serious, hardworking student. When she returned home she asked her mother to wake her very early the next morning as the Sheikh had promised a prize to whoever came to school before the rest. The girl went to bed. But she could not sleep. So she got up and put on her clothes and began to ready herself for school. Her mother heard her and said,

"It is much too early yet!"

"The world is full of light outside," replied her daughter.

"Moonlight," said the mother.

All the same, the girl got dressed, slipped on her new clogs, one of silver, one of gold, packed her notebook and pencil and set off for the schoolhouse.

When she got there, she found the door was locked. So she looked in at the window. What she saw was the Sheikh, her teacher, devouring a small boy. She spun round and fled. Running as fast as she could to get home she did not notice that the clog of silver had fallen off her foot. In her terror she was hoping that the Sheikh had not seen her. But the Sheikh had heard her anklets ringing.

That night while Sitt Yadab was asleep the Sheikh appeared to her and said:

"Sitt Yadab, O Sitt Yadab,
When you came, so bright and bold,
What did you see your teacher do
That made you lose your silver shoe
And run in just the one of gold?"

Her response was:

"I saw our Sheikh preparing tests
To help his students do their best."

The Sheikh said:

"Tell the truth or I will seize your father's camels."

She repeated:

"I saw our Sheikh preparing tests
To help his students do their best."

The Sheikh took her father's camels and vanished.

On the following day, Sitt Yadab did not go to school, saying that her head ached. That night the Sheikh appeared to her again asking:

"Sitt Yadab, O Sitt Yadab,
When you came, so bright and bold,
What did you see your teacher do
That made you lose your silver shoe
And run in just the one of gold?"

She answered:

"I saw our Sheikh preparing tests
To help his students do their best."

"Speak!" said the Sheikh, "or I'll take your father's sheep."

She said:

"I saw him praying and fasting,
Praising God, the Everlasting."

The Sheikh took her father's sheep and disappeared.

The next day, Sitt Yadab did not go to school, saying that her stomach hurt.

At night the Sheikh returned and asked:

"Sitt Yadab, O Sitt Yadab,
When you came, so bright and bold,
What did you see your teacher do
That made you lose your silver shoe
And run in just the one of gold?"

She said:

"I saw our Sheikh preparing tests

To help his students do their best."

"Go on," said the Sheikh, "or I will devour your mother and your father."

She said:

"I saw him praying and fasting,

Praising God the Everlasting."

The Sheikh took her parents and disappeared.

When it was morning, Sitt Yadab decided to escape into God's wide world so she would not meet the demon Sheikh again. She left her home and walked all day. Just as the sun was about to set, she came to a souk, or market. There she entered a grocer's shop and said to the owner:

"O Uncle, I have no one I can go to, no one to care for me. Please let me sleep here tonight and I will leave in the morning."

The grocer hesitated a little but then, seeing how exhausted she was, how pitiable and scared, he agreed to let her sleep in his shop. He gave her a round of bread and a jug of water, turned his key in the door and left. During the night the Sheikh appeared as before and asked:

"Sitt Yadab, O Sitt Yadab!

When you came, so bright and bold,

What did you see your teacher do

That made you lose your silver shoe
And run in just the one of gold?"
She said:
"I saw him praying and fasting
Praising God, the Everlasting."
"Speak up," said the Sheikh, "or I will ruin everything in sight."
She repeated:
"I saw him praying and fasting
Praising God, the Everlasting."
The Sheikh turned the shop upside down; he mixed the fat with the olive oil and the lentils with the wheat and the sugar with the rice then he left.

When the grocer unlocked his shop in the morning he found Sitt Yadab in tears. When he saw what had been done to his goods, he beat his head with his fists and called his fellow storekeepers to come and look. He declared that the girl was mad and drove her out into the street.

Walking and walking, Sitt Yadab came to another town. She went into a potter's shed and said to the potter:

"O Uncle, I have no one to go to and no one to care for me. Please let me sleep here tonight and I will go in the morning."

The potter hesitated at first, but then he agreed. He gave her a round of bread and a jug of water; he locked his shop and left.

The Sheikh came during the night and asked:
"Sitt Yadab, O Sitt Yadab,
When you came, so bright and bold,
What did you see your teacher do
That made you lose your silver shoe
And run in just the one of gold?"
She said:
"I saw him praying and fasting
Praising God, the Everlasting."
"If you don't speak further," said the Sheikh, "I will smash everything there is."
She repeated:
"I saw him praying and fasting
Praising God, the Everlasting."
The Sheikh broke the jars and jugs of earthenware and the cups and plates of finer ware and left.

When the potter unlocked his shed in the morning he found Sitt Yadab crying. When he saw what had been done to his wares, he began to shout and scream so that people gathered round. He yelled that Sitt Yadab was crazy and chased her away.

The girl walked on until she found herself by the prince's castle. She searched for food on the ground outside the castle wall, picking up scraps of bread and weeping as she ate. The prince who was looking out his window caught sight of her. He was struck by her beauty and sent one of his serving men to bring her into the palace. After she had been fed and her hunger stilled, she went to thank the prince for his kindness. He asked her for her story so she told him:

"I have no one to go to and there is no one to care for me. Time has swept me up in its stream: my people are dead and here I am, wandering from place to place."

The prince had been dazzled by her beauty and he was touched by her words. He decided to marry her. Wedding celebrations were arranged and Sitt Yadab became a princess living in the prince's palace. Soon she was pregnant and gave birth to a handsome boy as splendid as the moon. She forgot her troubles and the sufferings of her parents. But on the night after she gave birth, the Sheikh appeared to her once more. He asked:

"Sitt Yadab, O Sitt Yadab,
When you came, so bright and bold,
What did you see your teacher do
That made you lose your silver shoe
And run in just the one of gold?"
She said:
"In his hands he held the Holy Book
And on his face he had a saintly look."

"If you don't say more," said the Sheikh, "I'll snatch your son."

"The child is no dearer to me than my mother and my father," said the girl.

The Sheikh took the child, smeared Sitt Yadab's lips with blood and left.

The next day when the prince discovered that his son had vanished without a trace and he saw the blood on his wife's lips, he was overcome with sorrow and anger. He ordered Sitt Yadab to be confined to her quarters, and no one was to speak to her.

Days came and days went and the prince's heart softened towards his wife. He visited her in her rooms and asked her what had happened but she said nothing. For a second time, Sitt Yadab became pregnant, and this time she gave birth to a little girl. Again on the night after she gave birth, the Sheikh came to her and asked:

"Sitt Yadab, O Sitt Yadab,
When you came, so bright and bold,
What did you see your teacher do
That made you lose your silver shoe
And run in just the one of gold?"
She said:
"In his hands he held the Holy Book
And on his face he had a saintly look."

"If you don't tell," said the Sheikh, "I'll take your daughter."

"She is no dearer to me than my mother and my father," said Sitt Yadab.

The Sheikh took the child, stained the mother's lips with blood and left.

In the morning when the prince found that his baby daughter had disappeared and when he saw the blood on his wife's lips, he was convinced that she must be a ghoul. He ordered Sitt Yadab to be locked in her room and announced that no one was to speak to her.

Days came and days went and the prince decided to go on the pilgrimage to Mecca, the Hajj. He sent a serving girl to ask Sitt Yadab whether there was anything she wanted from there.

The serving woman entered Sitt Yadab's room and said:

"My master sends you greetings. He asks, what do you want him to bring you from the Hajj?"

Sitt Yadab said:

"Give your master my greetings. Tell him that I would like him to bring me the stone of patience and the knife of sorrow. Don't forget."

The prince was puzzled when the serving girl told him of Sitt Yadab's wish. Still, when he went on the Hajj he brought back the stone of patience and the knife of sorrow.

Sitt Yadab held the stone and began to cut its surface with the knife as she unburdened her story:

"O Stone of Patience! O Knife of Sorrow!

Help me to endure!

Our teacher the Sheikh,

God grant him good night and good morrow,

Took my father's camels and his sheep and I said nothing!

O Stone of Patience! O Knife of Sorrow!
Help me to endure!
Our teacher the Sheikh,
God grant him good night and good morrow,
Took my father and my mother and I said nothing!
O Stone of Patience! O Knife of Sorrow!
Help me to endure!
Our teacher, the Sheikh,
God grant him good night and good morrow,
Ruined grocer and potter, they called me mad, and
    I said nothing!
O Stone of Patience! O Knife of Sorrow!
Help me to endure!
Our teacher the Sheikh,
God grant him good night and good morrow,
Took my heart's lifeblood, my little son and daughter,
People thought me ghoul and monster,
And I said nothing!
O Solid Stone, lend me patience! O Sharp-edged Knife,
    help me to endure!"

Sitt Yadab wept as she etched with the knife a cut on the stone for each of her sorrows. She shed tears as she recited her refrain. She cried through the day and cried through the night. But, as darkness was lifting, the ground at her feet split open and the Sheikh appeared. He addressed her with these words:

"O Sitt Yadab, no human has existed
Who defied my orders or strength resisted
Until your patience and your tears,
For the first time in all my years,
Sapped my strength and conquered me!"

With that he returned the camels and the sheep, the father and the mother, and Sitt Yadab's little son and daughter. Then the Sheikh, her teacher, vanished.

Now Sitt Yadab's tears were tears of joy and all who were with her wept also.

A serving woman passing heard the sound of voices and looked in. She witnessed all that had taken place and brought the news to her master.

On entering Sitt Yadab's room, the prince beheld, with joy, his son and daughter. Clasping them to his heart he said:

"Yadab, O Yadab, my dear wife,
Will you tell me the story of your strange life."

She answered him:

"Rather, ask this Stone of Patience, it can tell the tale.
Patience taught me to bear every slight
Patience made the heaviest sorrows light
Patience is a gift from God, Who sees wrong and right.
I was silent. I did not sigh.
Now God has blessed me.
The return of dear parents and dear children is my reward."

Sitt Yadab was reinstated as a princess. She handed the Stone of Patience and the Knife of Sorrow to her daughter, advising her to keep them safe for they would give her strength when she had to endure in silence.

The parents arrived and the wedding celebrations were renewed; this was a marriage for which there were two rejoicings. The prince and Sitt Yadab then lived together in happiness and peace.

The bird has flown and is gone,
Goodnight to you every one.

BIR BRAMBIR

There was or there was not
In days that time forgot...
Shall we stay up and speak
Or go to bed and sleep?
Then let us begin with a prayer
For the Prophet, God's Messenger.

THERE WAS A MAN whose wife died and left him to look after their only daughter. In time the man remarried. Soon his second wife became pregnant and gave birth to a little girl. Now that she had a daughter of her own, the stepmother grew jealous of her husband's child. She favored her own daughter, giving her food that was tasty, words that were sweet, and tasks that were easy. Her husband's child was made to eat stale leftovers, hear harsh rebukes, and do all the heavy chores. So much did the woman dislike her husband's daughter that she was forever thinking how she might be rid of her. Then one day she called her and said:

"Go to Mother Ghoul and ask to borrow her sieve." Under her breath she added: "This time she will surely not come back."

The girl set off.

After she had walked a while, she noticed a date palm

with its trunk bent over. She went up to it and asked what the matter was.

"I am thirsty. Bring me some water," said the palm tree. The girl went to the stream and brought water to pour round the tree's roots. As soon as the date palm felt the water, its trunk straightened and it said:

"God willing, you will grow to be tall like me."

On walked the girl and soon she saw a rose that was all wilted.

"Why are you like this?" she asked.

"I am thirsty. Bring me some water," said the rose.

So the girl went to the stream and brought water to splash on the rose. When the rose had sipped the water its petals unfurled and it said:

"God willing, your cheeks will be rosy like mine."

The girl continued walking. On her way she passed by a horse kneeling on the ground. She asked what had happened. The horse said:

"I am thirsty. Bring me some water."

So the girl went to the stream and brought water for the horse to drink. When it had finished drinking, it stood up on its hooves and said:

"God willing, your hair will be as fine and as long as my mane."

The girl walked on until she reached Mother Ghoul's house.

She saw her sitting outside the door so she stopped in front of her and greeted her. Then she explained that her stepmother, her father's wife, had sent her to borrow a sieve.

"Before I let you have the sieve," said the Ghoul, "I want you to go into my house and make a mess and break the plates and wring the chickens' necks."

But once the girl was inside, she swept the house, washed the dishes, and fed the chickens. The Ghoul was delighted when she saw what the girl had done. She led her to the well and lowered her into it on a rope chanting:

"Bir Brambir
Deepest Well,
Hear my spell,
I am letting down a virtuous maiden
Send her back with treasures laden
For every coin that she may spend
Forty more you shall extend."

The girl emerged from the well covered with gold and with shining coins. The ghoul handed her the sieve and she went home.

Her stepmother saw her coming from afar. She saw how tall and slim she had become; how rosy her cheeks and how fine the hair falling to her shoulders. She saw the gold and the coins. All this only made her more jealous and more resentful.

Next day the stepmother gave her daughter the sieve and told her to hasten to the house of Mother Ghoul. She told her to give back the sieve and to ask the ghoul to do for her what she had done for her sister.

Off ran the daughter and went on running until she came to a date palm with its trunk bowed down. The tree tried to stop her and ask for water but the girl did not pause. The date palm said:

"God willing your skin will become spotted like mine."

On ran the girl. She passed by a withered rose that tried to stop her and ask for water but the girl took no notice. The rose said:

"God willing your body will be covered with thorns like mine."

On and on she ran. She ran past a horse kneeling on the ground. The horse tried to stop her and ask for water but the girl hurried on. The horse said:

"God willing, your feet will harden into hooves like mine."

The girl did not stop until she reached Mother Ghoul's house. She saw the ghoul sitting outside her door so she went up and gave her back the sieve. Then she asked her to do for her what she had done for her sister.

"Before I do for you what I did for your sister," said the Ghoul, "you must go into my house and make a mess and break the plates and wring the chickens' necks."

The girl went inside and messed up the house, smashed the dishes, and killed the chickens. When the ghoul saw what she had done she was furious. She led the girl to the well and dropped her into it chanting:

"Bir Brambir
Deepest Well
Hear my Spell
I am sending down an unkind child
Cover her with tails of donkeys wild
For every tail she plucks in her disgrace
Let forty more grow in its place."

The girl came out of the well with donkeys' tails all over her. That is how she went home.

Her mother saw her from afar: she saw her spotty skin full of thorns; her feet hardened into horse's hooves and, hanging from every part of her body, the tails of wild donkeys. The sight of her daughter in this condition filled the mother with such a swelling rage that she burst and fell down dead.

This is our story and we have told it
In your pocket you now can hold it.

THE GREEN BIRD

O NCE THERE WAS, or maybe there wasn't, a man who lived happily with his wife and two children, a boy and a girl. All continued well with him and his wife and son and daughter until his wife fell ill. On her deathbed, she said to her husband:

"Promise me that, after I am gone, you will not take another wife until our daughter is grown tall enough to wear my dress."

The husband gave his word and kissed his wife. Then she kissed her children goodbye and died.

Their nearest neighbor was a widow living by herself. She had heard about the husband's promise to his dying wife. She took needle and thread and a plateful of cakes and went next door. Her visit was a welcome surprise. She helped the children set the house in order and she gave them cake to eat. Before leaving, she threaded her needle and said to the girl:

"Come, my dear, let me fix your dress. The hem is sagging on one side."

The girl stood still while the neighbor turned up the bottom of the dress and stitched it on every side with her needle and thread.

After this, the neighbor made a habit of looking in on them. Every time she came, she would fold the hem a little and shorten the dress. Again and again she lifted the hem until a year went by. Then she said to the girl:

"My dear, your mother's dress fits you perfectly! You are a young woman now. Tell your father he must get married and make me his wife."

The girl was thrilled. She ran to her father saying:

"Dear Father, look! My mother's dress fits me now: I am a grown girl! It is time for you to get married."

"Marry?" exclaimed the father. "So whom should I marry?"

"Why, our neighbor, the woman next door! She loves us and we love her."

The father turned the thought over in his mind. He decided that this neighbor was a good woman; she would be a suitable wife for himself and a second mother to his children. He married her and she moved in to live with him and his daughter and little son. She continued to look after the two children and take care of the house and was indeed like a second mother to them.

Unfortunately, God would not bless this woman with a child of her own. She waited and hoped but never became pregnant. Her mood began to change. Instead of giving the two children a bath, she would give them a beating. Instead of looking after them, she would force them to work for her. Meanwhile, the husband did not notice that anything was different; he was delighted with the clean house and tasty meals.

One day the man said to his wife that he felt like a dish of tripe for his supper. He went to the market and bought some tripe for her to cook. Then he left to go to work, knowing that in the evening when he returned he would find his dinner ready.

The woman lit her cooking fire and trimmed the tripe and washed it and set it in a pot to stew. As it simmered, she would lift up the lid to take a mouthful and check how it tasted, then cover the pot and get on with her work. After the first mouthful she went back for a second; she covered the pot and returned to what she was doing. She did this a third time and continued interrupting her housework to take a taste until she had finished off all the tripe. When she looked into the pot and saw that she had eaten it all, she began to wail:

"Oh, what have I done? I am sunk! I swear my husband will kill me if he finds out!"

Then she had an idea. Seizing a knife she called the daughter and asked her to shout out to her little brother. But when the girl saw the knife in her stepmother's hand she was frightened. So this was her call:

"Hey! Little Brother, Hey!
I say, 'Come!' but stay away!
The water is on the boil
And the knife is sharp."

"What are you are saying, girl?" cried the stepmother.

"I am calling my brother, Aunt," the girl replied.

"Get going then," scolded the stepmother, "tell him to come right away!"

The girl raised her voice and called again:

"Hey! Little Brother, Hey!
I say, 'Come,' but stay away!
The water is on the boil
And the knife is sharp."

She returned and told her stepmother:

"I can't find him."

"On your way, now!" said the woman, "Bring him back immediately or I will surely kill you."

So the girl fetched her brother and he came home. The step-mother grabbed him and bathed him; then she slit his throat and stuffed him into the pot to stew as she had stewed the tripe.

The girl was in tears when she entered the house. She cried and cried and cried.

"Hush! Not a word out of you!" said the stepmother.

When the father came back from work, he went to check on the food to see if it was done. The water was boiling and the pot spoke up:

"The water has bubbled and the pot is uncovered
O Prophet, to whom God's message was delivered
How can the ways of Fate or time of Death be known?"

The father did not understand a word. When he went to take another look at the food and lifted the lid, he heard the tripe say:

"A dish of tripe is from the belly of a sheep

A cruel woman is not the wife you want to keep

How can the ways of Fate or time of Death be known?"

The father still understood nothing. He sat at the table and began to eat. He asked after his son:

"Where is the boy? Why is he not eating with us?"

"He ate already and went to bed," said the stepmother.

He asked his daughter:

"Why are you crying? And why are you not eating?"

"I have had enough," she said.

The father was hungry; he ate and ate, enjoying his fine dinner. He sucked on the bones and threw them out the window. When he was done, the girl fetched her mother's green headscarf and ran outside to gather up her brother's bones. She wrapped them in the green scarf and buried them in the cemetery. She wept and wept and wept, and then went home.

The days came and the days went. The girl was missing her brother. She went and dug up his grave. To her surprise, a bird with green, green feathers flew out from where the bones had been. He started to flutter around her, singing:

"I am the bird with feathers green,

No finer bird was ever seen.

My aunt was the butcher

My father the diner

Only my sister,

With her fond heart,

Picked up my bones
That were scattered apart
To bury them under a stone.
I am the Green Bird, free as air!
Flying here, flying everywhere!"

The girl was delighted to have found her brother again. Wherever she went, he followed, fluttering above her head and singing. Then, one day, he led the way to the blacksmith's shop and, singing his song, he asked for a handful of nails.

The townspeople were gathered in the cemetery for a funeral. The bird with green feathers hovered over the crowd and sang:

"I am the bird with feathers green
No finer bird was ever seen.
My aunt was the butcher,
My father the diner,
Only my sister
With her fond heart
Picked up my bones
That were scattered apart
To bury them under a stone.
I am the Green Bird, free as air!
Flying here, flying everywhere!"

The stepmother stiffened when she heard this. Everyone else was looking upwards astonished by the beauty of the bird and his green feathers. The bird, however, flew down to where the woman was standing and dropped the nails into her mouth, which had fallen open with horror. She died in an instant.

The funeral was interrupted, the women waved their scarves and everybody turned to the bird and said:

"Speak, Bird, speak again!"

"I will not speak or sing," said the bird, "until this man here opens his mouth."

The father opened his mouth and the bird repeated his song:

"I am the bird with feathers green,

No finer bird was ever seen.

My aunt was the butcher,

My father the diner,

Only my sister,

With her fond heart,

Picked up my bones,

That were scattered apart

To bury them under a stone.

I am the Green Bird, free as air,

Flying here, flying everywhere!"

He threw the nails into his father's mouth and the man died instantly.

As he had done before, the bird kept fluttering above his sister's head. When they were alone again, the girl said:

"Come, Brother, let us get away from this place. God's wide earth is open before us."

She set off walking and walking, with the bird flying overhead or resting on her shoulder whenever he was tired. Eventually, they came to a spring and the bird said:

"Sister, I am thirsty."

The girl went to the water and asked:

"O Spring, if my brother drinks your water, will he still be a bird, unchanged?"

"If he drinks my water," said the spring, "he will turn into a cat and scratch his sister."

"Drink, Brother," said the girl, "drink, if you are thirsty!"

"No, Sister, I will not drink," said the brother.

So the girl went on walking and walking, with the bird following after, until they came to a second spring and the bird said:

"Sister, I am thirsty."

The sister asked:

"O Spring, if my brother drinks your water, will he still be a bird, unchanged?"

"If your brother drinks my water," said the spring, "he will turn into a dog and bite his sister."

"Drink, Brother," said the girl, "drink, if you are thirsty!"

"No, Sister, I will not drink," said the bird.

The girl continued to walk and walk and the bird went on fluttering above her until they came to a well and again the bird said that he was thirsty.

"O Well," asked the girl, "If my brother drinks your water, will he still be a bird, unchanged?"

"If he drinks my water," the well replied, "he will turn into a gazelle and follow in his sister's footsteps."

"Drink your fill, Brother," said the girl, "Drink!"

The green bird drank and was transformed into a gazelle wearing a golden chain around his neck.

Here they rested. And here is where the king's son had gone out hunting with his companions. When he saw the girl sitting by herself with a gazelle at her side, he said:

"My friends, you may hunt whatever you wish, but this catch is mine."

He went up to the girl and asked her to tell him her name.

"I am called Nhud," she said.

He asked her what she was doing there all by herself, and she explained that her parents were dead, she was their only daughter, and she had no other family. So the king's son took her with him to his palace with the gazelle following after. It was not long before the prince decided to marry the girl. She agreed on one condition: that the gazelle would always remain with her. So they were married. The girl lived in the palace and soon she was pregnant. However, her husband's first cousins felt slighted and were jealous. They complained to each other:

"Where on earth did he find this stranger, and here we

are, his own first cousins, with a greater right to him than all others!"

One day, when the king's son was away, the cousins said:

"Nhud, we're going on a picnic. Why don't you join us?"

She went with them. But this was a trick that the cousins had devised because they wanted to be rid of her. They had placed a straw mat over the mouth of a well. Then, sitting down in a circle on the edge of the mat, they invited Nhud to sit in the middle as part of a game they all would play. They told her:

"You have to sit in the middle. That is the rule of the game."

The girl settled herself in the middle of the mat. The gazelle was standing nearby watching. Suddenly the cousins stood up, all at the same time. This caused the girl slip down into the well, taking the mat with her. As for the cousins, they left and ran off. But the gazelle remained by the well shedding tears. He wept and wept until it was dark, then returned to the palace alone.

When the king's son came home, he asked his mother where his wife was. She told him that his wife had gone back to wherever she had come from.

"Tell me where she is!" he insisted.

"She went on a picnic with your uncle's daughters," said his mother. "Then she disappeared. She must have run away."

The prince found this very strange. He had to find her.

Meanwhile, the gazelle began to look for any stray crust of

bread or piece of fruit lying around, which he could carry in his mouth and, running to the well, throw to his sister. They say, "Rather count the eggs you break into the pan than the months of a woman with child." In time, at the bottom of the well, Nhud gave birth to a boy. The gazelle continued to drop scraps of food down to her, starving himself and wasting away. He would sit near the wellhead talking to his sister:

"My own dear Sister, kind in word and deed
Pity your brother grown thin as river reeds
With you I feasted on white sesame and sweet walnuts
Now my meals are kitchen garbage and dry bread crusts."

And she would reply:

"O Little Gazelle, my Brother dear,
Wherever I am you follow near
You saw their trick and know my plight
I live in darkness like the night
As if a whale has swallowed me
Only my long hair now covers me
The prince's son sleeps on my arm
God keep us both from every harm!"

As the days passed, the king's son could see that his wife's gazelle was wasting away. He began to give it better food with his own hand, and he noticed that the gazelle was not eating what he was given but carried in his mouth and ran with it out of the palace. So the king's son followed. He was standing behind a tree, watching, as the gazelle trotted up to the well. He heard him speak:

"My own dear Sister, kind in word and deed
Pity your brother grown thin as river reeds
With you I feasted on white sesame and sweet walnuts
Now my meals are kitchen garbage and dry bread crusts."

Then the king's son heard his wife's voice rising out of the well:

"O Little Gazelle, my Brother dear,
Wherever I am you follow near
You saw their trick and know my plight
I live in darkness like the night
As if a whale has swallowed me
Only my long hair now covers me
The prince's son sleeps on my arm
God keep us both from every harm!"

The king's son rushed to the well and rescued his wife and child. When he had brought them back to the palace, the girl told him her story from beginning to end, starting with how her stepmother killed her little brother, to how his bones turned into the Green Bird, and then into the gazelle now standing by their side.

The girl and king's son lived long and happily together and they were never parted from the gazelle with the golden chain around his neck.

THE SINGING TURD

O Lord, Exalted One!
Creator, who shaped us from top to toe!
Hear my cries of longing, my cries of woe!
Grant me a child to carry and call my own.

THIS WAS THE WOMAN'S DAILY PRAYER. Day after day, she pleaded with God to bless her with a little daughter. But God did not respond to her petitions. Then, one night, worn down by despair, the woman declared that she would accept God's blessing in whatever form it came.

"O Lord, Exalted One!
Who hears our every word
Grant me a child, a little one,
Even if she is just a turd."

God fulfilled her wish. She became pregnant and after nine months she gave birth to a turd. Happy to be a mother, the woman picked up her little daughter and placed her in a bowl of cut crystal, which she set on a shelf in the bathhouse. She pushed back the window shutters so the child could look outside and not feel lonesome.

The daughter liked to sing and she had a voice that could move the world.

One day the son of the sultan happened to pass by the window and heard her singing. Her voice entered his heart.

When he returned to the palace, he told his mother that he wished her to ask for the hand of the singer in marriage.

The sultan's wife went to the house, taking with her a golden platter heaped with jewels. She knocked on the door and entered. She explained that she had come to ask for the hand of the singer with the beautiful voice as a wife for her son:

"I come courting my intentions most serious.

Rejection will cause me sorrow most grievous."

The mother was confused by this request and she said regretfully:

"But I have no girls suitable for marriage."

The sultan's wife persisted, guessing that the mother was hiding her daughter because of some defect in the girl.

"I will accept your daughter as she is," she said.

"But I do not have any marriageable girls," repeated the mother.

The sultan's wife insisted:

"We will welcome your daughter whatever her condition. My son is determined to marry her."

"May God judge us and show mercy as we face this trouble that has come upon us," said the mother. And, without another word, she accepted the tray of jewels.

When the guest had returned to her palace, the woman went to the bathhouse to tell her daughter the news:

"O my child, my dear one! You have to hurry and bathe because the Sultan's son has chosen you to be his wife."

The daughter began to sing:
"I have no hair to brush,
I have no limbs to wash,
I have no beauty to display.
If the Sultan's son comes courting, alas,
What words are there for me to say?"

Just then, as she was singing her plaintive song, a man walked by the window. He looked inside to see who possessed a voice of such beauty.

Now this man had a strange history. Years before, he had been stricken with a mysterious disease that caused a large swelling to cover his face. The doctors were puzzled and declared it incurable. The man, for whom there was no cure, had been wandering about the streets as if to bid the world goodbye. When he heard the beautiful voice he was eager to discover who the singer was.

So he looked through the bathhouse window, but all he saw was a turd on a shelf sitting in a crystal bowl and singing. This made him explode with laughter. She was singing and he was laughing. He continued to laugh as he went on his way. He entered his house still laughing. He laughed and laughed so hard that the swelling on his face burst and disappeared.

The man had seven beautiful sisters living with him in his house. The sisters had refused marriage and instead had devoted themselves to constant prayer for their brother's recovery. When they heard their brother laughing, they rushed to find out the reason why. They could see that he had been cured and they asked him how. So he told them all that he had seen and heard. The sisters were overjoyed by their brother's healing. They wanted to listen to the singer and see her for themselves. They dressed in their outdoor clothes and stood beneath the bathhouse window. They heard the beautiful voice singing:

"I have no hair to brush,

I have no limbs to wash,

I have no beauty to display,

If the Sultan's son comes courting, alas,

What words are there for me to say?"

When the sisters saw who the singer was, they decided that, as she had cured their brother, so too must she be helped. They prayed fervently, asking God to grant their wishes on her behalf:

The first sister said: Let her have a fine body like mine.

The second sister said: Let her have a full breast like mine.

The third sister said: Let her have long hair like mine.

The fourth sister said: Let her have clear eyes like mine.

The fifth sister said: Let her have fair skin like mine

The sixth sister said: Let her have my wisdom.

The seventh sister said: Let her have my wit.

Just then the Sultan's wife came to visit. She asked:

"Why do you keep your daughter hidden away? I want to see your singer with the beautiful voice!"

Without responding the mother went to the bathhouse and knocked on the door. When she went in she could not believe her eyes. She let out a scream of joy. She saw her daughter transformed into a shapely young woman, radiant as the sun, with a beauty that could tell the moon to set so she might sit in its place. She hailed her:

"God's blessing upon you!
Blessings all around you!
My child is young and fair of form
Like noonday's sun she's bright and warm!
She can tell the moon to go away
And in its place herself hold sway."

Such was the mother's joyous ululation as her daughter stepped out. Meanwhile the sultan's wife looked at the girl and thought:

"This must be the most beautiful bride in the whole world!"

As for the sultan's son, when he saw that she was as enchanting as her voice, he fell in love all over again. So they were married. All who knew them wished them well and they lived out their lives in happiness and delight.

May your lives be as happy, God willing! Inshallah!

THE MOUSE THAT WANTED
A HUSBAND

To tell a tale I am most willing.
My daughter back and forth is running
There's a gecko on the bathhouse ceiling
Never mind it does not matter
We can reach it with a ladder
My daughter is fretful and worried
I'll tell her the tale of a mouse that got married.

THIS IS THE STORY OF THE LITTLE MOUSE that wanted a husband.

Every morning and every night the little mouse said to her mother:

"Mother dear, I want to get married!"

And her mother would reply:

"Dear child, wait a while, be patient. You are far too young for marriage."

So it went, day after day, until one day the little mouse told her mother:

"Mother, I have decided! I am going to get married today!"

So her mother said:

"Go and sit up by the main road and look out for a passerby who pleases you. Then say: 'Would you like to have me as your bride?'"

The little mouse washed herself and bathed; she combed her hair and put on the most beautiful dress she owned. She sat by the side of the road and waited and waited. A camel came along and stopped in front of her. He asked:

"O Little Mouse, O Mousekin! What are you doing here?"

She answered:

"I am looking for a husband."

The camel proudly stretched his neck and said:

"I am the perfect bridegroom. Will you have me?"

The little mouse said:

"Put your gold inside my sleeve
I'll have to ask my mother's leave."

Back to the house she ran, calling:

"Mother, Mother!
His eyes are large, so large
His head is large, so large
His hooves are large, so large
All of him is O so very large!"

"Why, that is the camel!" cried her mother. "What a calamity! If he should fall on you, he'd crush you to death."

The little mouse ran back to the road and said to the camel:

"My mother won't hear of it!"

She gave him the gold, which she had knotted into the end of her wide sleeve, and the camel went on his way.

The little mouse sat and waited and waited until a donkey came along. He stopped in front of her and asked:

"O Little Mouse, O Mousekin! What are you doing here?"
She said:
"I am looking for a husband."
The donkey brayed loudly and said:
"I am the ideal bridegroom. Will you have me?"
The little mouse said:
"Put your gold inside my sleeve
I'll have to ask my mother's leave."
The donkey placed the gold in the end of her sleeve and the
little mouse hurried home to tell her mother:
"Mother, Mother!
His eyes are big, so big!
His head is big, so big
His hooves are big, so big!
All of him is O so very big!"
"That is the donkey!" said her mother. "What bad luck! If
he should fall on you he would crush you to death."

The little mouse ran back to the road and said to the
donkey:
"My mother says, 'No!'"
She returned the gold she had tied in her sleeve and the
donkey went on his way.

The little mouse sat by the road and waited and waited.
Then a handsome mouse came along and stood before her
and asked:
"O Little Mouse, O Mousekin! What are you doing here?"

She answered:

"I am looking for a husband."

He said:

"I'll be your bridegroom! Will you have me?"

She replied:

"Put your gold inside my sleeve

I'll have to ask my mother's leave."

Then home she ran and shouted to her mother:

"Mother, Mother!

His eyes are small and bright

His head is just my height

His paws are neat and slight

All of him is O so very right!"

"That is your uncle's son, your first cousin," said her mother. "Yes, you may marry him! You have my blessing!"

The little mouse skipped all the way to the road and told the mouse:

"My mother says, 'Yes!'"

"Then let us get married!" said the mouse.

"No!" said the little mouse. "First we must spend some of the gold on wedding clothes."

So they went and bought their wedding finery.

"Now can we get married?" asked the mouse.

"No!" said the little mouse, "First I'd like to take a wedding bath."

"And after that will we marry?" he asked.

"We'll marry after that," she said.

"What would you like for the wedding feast?" he asked.

"Two cakes of kibbeh," she said, "that you can balance on your nose, two meat dumplings that you can carry in each ear, and a ball of cheese that you can roll in front of you when you come."

In a neighboring house there was a banquet and there the handsome mouse went to get what the little mouse wanted.

The little mouse, meanwhile, went to the well to have her bath. She swam and splashed and laughed for joy but when she wanted to climb out again she found she could not do it. She tried and tried but was unable to get herself out of the well. She began to shout as loudly as she could to let the people hear her. She called out for help but no one heard. Then a man rode by on his way to the neighbor's banquet. When he stopped at the well to water his donkey, he heard a voice calling:

"O rider on a fine horse riding

Your harness bells merrily jingling

To the prince of princes go and tell

That the fairest of the fair slipped and fell

And now awaits him at the bottom of the well.

Do this and don't forget

Or you'll have reason for regret:

When you try to rise and stand upright

Your bottom to the mat will be stuck tight."

The man mounted his donkey and trotted off to the banquet. He ate and drank and danced and sang then sat down to rest on the straw matting that covered the floor. He forgot all that had happened before. Then when he wanted to get up again he found his bottom was stuck to the mat. His friends laughed and he remembered the well; he laughed too as he told his friends:

"When I was on my way here I stopped at the well to water my donkey. The fairest of the fair was in the well! She was looking for the prince of princes! She called out to me:

'O rider, on a fine horse riding
Your harness bells merrily jingling
To the prince of princes go and tell
That the fairest of the fair slipped and fell
And now awaits him at the bottom of the well.
Do this and don't forget
Or you'll have reason for regret:
When you try to rise and stand upright
Your bottom to the mat will be stuck tight.'"

The mouse heard all this and guessed that the fairest of the fair was the little mouse and he himself was the prince of princes. Quickly he jumped and quickly he grabbed two cakes of kibbeh and balanced them on his nose, two meat dumplings and carried them in his ears, and a round of cheese to roll before him. Then he ran and ran, hopping from stone to stone and leaping from rock to rock, until he reached the well. Dropping the food on the ground, he cried:

"O Little Mouse, O Mousekin, what do you want me to do?"

"Save me! Rescue me!" she said. "Pull me out of the well!"

"Shall I reach down my paw?" he asked.

"No," she said.

"Shall I stretch down my leg?" he asked.

"No," she said.

"Shall I bend down my ear?" he asked.

"No!" she said.

"Shall I let down my tail?" he asked.

"Yes!" she said, "Yes, let down your tail."

The mouse let his tail hang down and the little mouse took firm hold of it; he pulled and pulled until she came up out of the well. The mouse was overjoyed and the little mouse was happy. They danced in the light of the sun. They wore their wedding clothes. They feasted on their wedding meal. They were married and had many little baby mice.

The bird has taken flight
God grant you a good night.

THE DRINKING FOUNTAIN

There was or there was not…
No tale is worthy of listeners generous and honorable,
Without first invoking God the Almighty and the Merciful…

T HERE ONCE WAS A KING who had a daughter. She was his only child and he loved her dearly and indulged her excessively. Then one night in his sleep he had a dream in which he saw himself kissing the hand of his son-in-law, his daughter's husband. He woke up angry and was furious at his daughter. He said to his wife:

"Have the girl taken to the palace of isolation. Do it today, don't wait till tomorrow. Do it now!"

The mother tried to argue with him:

"Listen to me, dear husband! Lighten up, dear one! Have a heart!"

But it was no use. The mother was forced to confine her daughter as the king commanded.

So it was that the girl came to spend her days in a palace apart that had no window or terrace to the outside and with only her maidservant to keep her company. She woke up alone, took her meals by herself, and went to sleep in her lonely bed. The servant girl would look in from time to time and her mother would steal a moment to pass by and check on her and then hurry home. But otherwise the girl was left to herself. She was bored by the sameness of her life. The loneliness oppressed her: she could no longer endure the isolation or wait for it to end.

When her mother next came to see her, the girl said:

"Mother dear, I am tired of this dull life. It is depressing to be alone all day. This banishment is unbearable. I can't wait for it to end."

Her mother put her arms around her but she said that she didn't know what she could do to change the orders given by her husband, the king.

"I will deal with this myself," said the girl. "Only give me a set of my father's clothes, one of my father's horses, and a saddlebag filled with money!"

"But where are you planning to go, my dearest?" her mother asked. "I fear for you."

"Trust me, Mother, and do not worry!" replied the girl, "God's earth is spacious and I want to leave. I can't stay here any longer."

Her mother brought the clothes and the horse and the saddlebag full of money. The girl dressed herself in her father's clothes, mounted his horse, and tied on the saddlebag. Then she kissed her mother and her maidservant and rode off.

She traveled without pausing until she had gone a long distance from her father's kingdom. When she finally stopped, she found herself in wild and desolate country with no one near but God above and the green grass below. Here she reined in her horse and dismounted. She drank from a nearby stream, watered her horse, and tied it to a tree. Then she stretched out on the ground and slept.

It was close to sunset when she woke up. She looked around and couldn't believe her eyes. "Am I dreaming or is this real?" she asked herself. What she saw before her was a strange building – as people like to say: "neither in the earth implanted nor from the sky suspended." Both she and her horse were hungry, so she decided to go inside, hoping to find something to eat. She stepped cautiously and when she stood on the threshold she announced:

"I am a traveler at your door!"

Then she called out to the people of the house:

"O masters of this house! Hey, masters of this house!"

There was no reply, so she entered. Near the doorway, there was a well-equipped stable, where she led her horse and fed it and watered it. Next, she went into the kitchen and found food and drink ready for someone to cook it: every kind of vegetable, meat, and fruit, sorted and arranged for cooking. The girl was delighted. She rolled up her sleeves and set to work. When she was done she cleaned and tidied the kitchen, then ladled the food she had cooked onto plates she found there. She took something to eat for herself, then joined her horse in the stable.

"I'll sleep here tonight," she said to herself, "and tomorrow I'll go."

The next day when she went into the kitchen she saw that the dishes had been emptied and again there was food laid out to be cooked. So she prepared it, dished it onto the plates, and had a meal herself. Then she cleaned and tidied the kitchen and returned to the stable to sleep, saying to herself: "I'll sleep here tonight and tomorrow I'll be off."

She spent the night in the stable and in the morning, when she went into the kitchen for the third time, she saw that the dishes were empty as before and everything readied for cooking. However, when she rolled up her sleeves to begin her work, the door flung wide open and an ancient man entered, venerable in appearance, with a beard down to his belt.

The girl was startled and quickly crouched under the table to hide. She heard the old man's voice saying:

"I sense a stranger in the place!
If it is a boy he will be a son to me,
If a girl, my daughter,
If a man, my brother,
If a woman, she will be my sister.
Whoever you may happen to be
Come out and show yourself to me!"

The girl was frightened and tried to run away but the old man saw her. He thought she was a boy because she was wearing her father's clothes and he called to her:

"O my son, my dear one!"

She corrected him and told him that she was a girl:

"No, Father," she said, "I am a maiden pure and untouched."

"Welcome, O my daughter, my dear one!" said the old man.

And so the girl lived with him as if she were his daughter and as if the old man were her father. Every day she would keep house and prepare the meals and then, in the afternoon, she would sit at the window with her spindle, twisting wool into yarn.

One day she saw an ostrich that belonged to the sultan's son in the palace garden next door. She greeted it from her window:

"Good evening to you, O ostrich, pet of the sultan's son!"

"A pleasant evening to you too, O daughter of the ghoul!" replied the ostrich and it went on to recite:

"O ghoul's daughter,

How fair your face and form

How fine your twist of yarn

Today the ghoul is raising you and feeding you

Tomorrow he will be roasting you and eating you!"

The girl was alarmed to hear this. She listened to the ostrich's warning but said nothing. She went to her room in silence and took to her bed. She would not eat or drink. She became thin and weak and her face lost all color. Seeing the state she was in, the old man asked:

"Dear heart, what has been happening to you?"

The girl did not respond. The old man persisted and continued to question her until she told him how she had seen the ostrich of the sultan's son. She repeated to him what the bird had said:

"It claimed that you are raising me and fattening me in order to devour me!"

The old man gave her this advice:

"If the ostrich recites the same words to you again tomorrow, tell it that I am feeding you and raising you so that the sultan's son may marry you."

The girl recovered her strength on hearing this. The following day she took her spindle and sat at the window spinning and waiting. As soon as she caught sight of the ostrich in the garden she greeted it:

"Good evening, O ostrich of the sultan's son!"

"Good evening to you too, O daughter of the ghoul," said the ostrich, adding:

"O ghoul's daughter,
How fair your face and form
How fine your twist of yarn,
Today the ghoul is raising you and feeding you

Tomorrow he will be roasting you and eating you!"
This time the girl was unafraid and answered boldly:
"He wants to feed me and raise me
So people may see me and praise me
And the sultan's son will ask my hand in marriage.
Then with your feathers I'll make my bed
And with your blood draw patterns red
Then with your flesh shall guests be fed
On my wedding day!"

When it heard the girl's boast, the ostrich shook with rage and began plucking its own feathers in frustration, scattering them on the ground. For several days they continued with the same exchange: the girl bidding the ostrich good evening and the ostrich ending by pulling out its feathers. Soon the sultan's son noticed the sorry shape of his bird. He saw the feathers covering the ground, so he asked:

"O ostrich, my pet, what is ailing you?"

The bird told how it had seen the girl spinning at her window and how it had warned her about the ghoul. And how, in response, the girl had dared to boast that she was going to marry the sultan's son.

"What time of day does this girl appear?" asked the sultan's son.

"She comes in the afternoon," said the ostrich, "and sits at the window and spins."

The sultan's son decided to see for himself. He was impatient for the hours to pass until afternoon. When it was the time for the girl to sit at the window and spin, he hid where he could watch her without being seen. He observed the ostrich passing by the window.

"Good evening to you, O ostrich of the sultan's son," said the girl.

"Good evening to you too, O daughter of the ghoul," replied the ostrich and said:

"O ghoul's daughter,
Great beauty you have and elegance
And sweet is the sound of your spindle
Tomorrow the ghoul his fire will kindle
To roast you
And eat you
And rid us of your presence."
To which the girl responded:
"No!
He has saved me from harm and from distress
He allows no speck of dust to touch my dress.
Tomorrow the sultan's son I'll wed
And with your feathers make my bed."

Again the ostrich was enraged and pulled at its feathers till they fell on the ground.

As for the sultan's son, one look and he was smitten with love for the girl. He found himself thinking about her both night and day. She was on his mind even while he ate and while he drank. In the end he went to his mother and said:

"O my Mother, I beg you, go and ask for the girl's hand in marriage!"

"What are you saying?" his mother exclaimed. "Do you expect me to ask for the hand of a girl from that strange quarter? From a place where we saw no builder building, or plasterer plastering, or painter painting, as the walls of the house rose up!"

But the young man was determined and he pestered his mother until she conceded and set a date to visit the girl.

The night before the visit, the old man told the girl:

"My child, tomorrow some people from the sultan's palace will be coming here. Welcome them politely and hospitably but when they offer you a platter filled with jewels, lay it aside without a second glance. And when you take their outer wraps, hang the clothes on the ropes above them. Then, after you have done your duty by them for a couple of hours, pull the ropes in such a way that each wrap falls into its owner's lap."

The next day, the girl prepared herself for the visitors from the sultan's palace. She made sure that the ropes the old man had mentioned were in place, and waited for the guests.

The party finally arrived: the sultan's wife accompanied by a number of women from the palace, bringing with them the gift of a platter heaped with jewels.

The girl welcomed the visitors and thanked them for their gift. Then she called a servant girl to put the platter away on a shelf and continued to entertain her guests as if nothing of significance had taken place. This annoyed the palace women. They were irritated by the girl's behavior and wondered, "How can she not be impressed by our gift of jewelry?" But they did not show what they were feeling.

The girl took good care of her guests, offering them coffee and sweetmeats and conversing with them politely, so that the time passed quickly and after two hours, the sultan's wife and her women were still sitting with her. At that point the girl pulled the rope that let fall each woman's wrap into her lap. The women understood that this was a signal that the visit was over and it was time for them to leave.

The sultan's wife could not contain her anger as she hastened back to the palace followed by her women. They were all puzzled by the girl's behavior.

The sultan's son was waiting on tenterhooks for his mother's return and ran out to meet the women saying:

"Tell me: How did it go? What do you think? Did you see her, Mother? Don't you like her?"

His mother replied:

"Likable she is and pleasant and kind and well bred, and also beautiful, I'll admit! But she did offend us on two counts."

"What did she do?" asked the youth.

His mother described to him how the girl had dismissed their gift of jewelry and had it put aside on a shelf. But her son's reaction was:

"She must have far costlier jewelry than that or she would not have cast your gift aside!"

Then his mother told him how after they had sat with her for two hours she had caused each of their wraps to fall into their laps. The son responded:

"She was a proper hostess to you and there was no need to linger beyond two hours!"

When eventually the palace decided to make a formal request for the girl's hand in marriage, the old man said:

"Dear child, tomorrow the palace will be sending a party to ask for your hand in marriage. Welcome them hospitably but put the gift of wedding jewels by the fireplace. After half an hour pull the rope to let them have their wraps."

So when the palace women arrived, the girl conducted herself as on the previous occasion except that this time she placed the palace gifts by the hearth and pulled the rope holding the visitors' coats after a mere half-hour.

Again, the women did not betray their feelings. But once they were outside and on their way back to the palace, they gave vent to their disappointment, buzzing with complaints and muttering to each other.

The sultan's son who had been waiting to hear the news was surprised by the mood of the delegation.

"What happened?" he asked.

Talking all at the same time, the women said:

"She insulted us!"

"She made fun of us!"

"She did not like us!"

"She spoke to us without any warmth!"

"This time she treated us worse than the time before!"

"She did nothing wrong!" insisted the sultan's son. "The first time she welcomed you as guests and strangers. Today she knew that you were asking for her in marriage so how could she treat you as before."

"Well," said the women, "we refuse to be her escorts on your wedding day or bring her in procession to your palace! Ask someone else to do the honors!"

"I shall go and bring her myself!" declared the sultan's son.

Meanwhile, the girl was bubbling with joy as she made ready for the day of her wedding. The old man came to her once again to offer his advice:

"Listen carefully to what I have to say, my child," he said. "Don't forget that you arrived here a king's daughter, riding your father's horse and wearing your father's clothes, carrying a saddlebag full of gold. When you are married, do not give your husband leave to speak with you until he has met one condition."

"What condition is that?" asked the girl.

So the old man explained:

"Tell your husband that you will be ready to speak to him on one condition – you will talk to him only after he has built a public drinking fountain in your name and placed your portrait above the water spout. In addition he must appoint two sentries to keep watch at the fountain. And if they see a man weeping and grieving after coming to drink they are to take him to the prison and inform the sultan's son. Tell your husband that you will know what to do then."

The girl guessed what the old man had in mind and thanked him for his instructions. She was longing to see her parents again.

"I shall climb to the top of the minaret to see you go to your new home in your husband's house," said the old man. "And when you leave this place my soul will depart also."

"No! No!" protested the girl, "Then I'd rather not get married!"

"It is time for your wedding procession," said the old man. "The sultan's son is on his way. Go to him! Live your life! May God grant you happiness and good fortune!"

The old man embraced the girl as she stood in her bridal finery and kissed her. And when the sultan's son came for her, the old man handed her to him with God's blessing. Then, from the top of the minaret, he watched as the sultan's son led his bride to the palace. When the girl turned one last time to look back at the minaret, she saw a light that grew fainter with every step she took.

Everyone in the city joined in the wedding celebrations: eating and drinking and dancing and singing! The palace women were there and the sultan's family and friends – even the ostrich of the sultan's son took part! The festivities did not end until the night became day!

When all the guests had gone and the bride and groom were alone with each other, the sultan's son wanted to sit with his wife and talk, but she stepped away saying:

"There is one condition that must be met before we may speak with each other."

He asked what that was and she told him that she wanted him to build a public drinking fountain and place her portrait above the water spout. He was to appoint two sentries to keep watch nearby. If they saw someone come to drink at the fountain and burst into tears, or sob or grieve, they were to take him down into the prison and report to the sultan's son. The sultan's son was to inform her and she would know what to do next.

The sultan's son met her condition: he built the drinking fountain with her portrait above the water and he appointed two sentries to keep watch nearby.

In his own kingdom, the girl's father began to miss his daughter. As the expression has it: "When gone are the fumes of drinking, regained are the powers of thinking." The king was remembering with regret how he had commanded the girl to be shut up in the palace of isolation and that he had not visited her since. He missed her.

"Dear lady," he said to his wife, "'Gone are the fumes of drinking; regained are the powers of thinking!' I am missing my daughter whom I banished to the palace of isolation. I want to see her."

"Dear husband," said his wife, "Your daughter left a long time ago. She took a horse from your stable and a suit of your clothes and I gave her a saddlebag full of gold. She rode off and I don't know where she has landed."

The king was heartbroken and filled with remorse. He said:

"I will go and look for her and will not come back until I have found her!"

His wife embraced him and wished him success in his quest.

The very next day, the king summoned his vizier and the two men disguised themselves as wandering dervishes and started on their way. They traveled here and there, "one place receiving them and another sending them away." The journey was long and the weather was hot. They were constantly thirsty and looking for drinking water. So it happened that one day they were led to the fountain that the sultan's son had built for his wife.

As the king cupped his hands and bent down to drink, he thought his eyes were deceiving him; for there, shimmering in the water he held in his palm, was the image of his daughter! He looked up and realized that it was the reflection of her portrait hanging above the water spout. At the sight, he sank onto the stone ledge of the fountain, holding his head between his hands and sobbing. The vizier rushed to comfort him but before he could finish a sentence the two sentries fell upon both dervishes, the king and his vizier, arrested them and threw them into prison. Two days passed before the sentries informed the sultan's son and two more days passed before the sultan's son remembered to tell his wife.

As soon as the young woman heard the news, she asked the sultan's son, her husband, to release the two men from prison; to have them taken to the bathhouse and bathed, then to the barber and shaved, after which they were to be brought to the palace for a meal. She herself would prepare the food.

When the sultan's son went down to the prison the next day and ordered the cell to be unlocked, the king and his vizier kissed his hands, first one and then the other.

"We are devout dervishes, your Majesty," they said. "What have we done to be imprisoned?"

The sultan's son apologized, and after they had bathed and shaved, he invited them to his palace to dine with him at his table.

When all the palace men gathered round the table, the king was made to sit in a chair that his daughter had designated for him. She wanted to observe her father through a peephole in the ceiling above the chair. She had cooked the king's favorite meal that she and her mother used to make for him every Friday. Through the opening in the ceiling the girl was watching closely. As soon as her father had tasted the first mouthful, his eyes welled with silent tears. On her part, the girl was crying too and one of her tears fell onto her father's hand. So the sultan's son said to the king:

"Let us go to the upper chambers. I have some questions for you about the architecture of the building."

So up went the sultan's son with the two dervishes, the king and his vizier, to where his wife was waiting for them. The sultan's son introduced the guests, telling his wife:

"These are two wandering dervishes." And to the men he said: "This is my wife!"

"But she my own daughter!" cried the dervish who was the king. "Come, dear child!"

He pressed her to his chest and kissed her many times. Then he explained the whole story:

"Dearest daughter, I once had a dream in which I saw myself kissing the hand of my son-in-law. It angered me and, because of the dream, I wrongfully punished you and also made your mother and myself miserable, separated from you for so long.

And look: today I not only kissed the hand of my son-in-law but his other hand too. I kissed both his hands!"

The news was sent to the girl's mother and there was happiness in every heart.

> *Then the son of the Sultan and the daughter of the King*
> *Lived in ease and plenty showered with blessings*
> *God sweeten the days of all who heard this storytelling.*

THURAYA WITH THE
LONG, LONG HAIR

It was or was not so
It happened long ago.
But first, an invocation:
The Prophet, Full Moon of Perfection.

THERE ONCE WERE THREE SISTERS, Fatima, Khadija, and Thuraya. They lived in a modest little house with their only brother. The brother went away to work all day and the young women stayed at home by themselves.

One day a beggar came to their door and knocked:

"May God give you plenty! Give this poor man something to eat."

Khadija said:

"Get up, Fatima, give him something!"

The beggar said:

"No! Please, I don't want my fate decided by Fatima!"

So Thuraya said:

"Get up, Khadija, you give him something!"

The beggar said:

"No! Please, I don't want to be kidded by Khadija!"

So Fatima said:

"Get up, Thuraya!"

"Yes!" said the beggar, "my heart and soul will thrive with Thuraya!"

Thuraya went to hand him a round of bread. But "a beggar's arm is short." As the young woman stepped towards him, the beggar backed off step-by-step until he had drawn her away from the others. Then he picked her up, flung her over his shoulder, and fled. He rose into the air and flew, soaring higher and higher.

"What can you see, Thuraya?" he asked.

"I see only clouds girdling the sky."

He flew still higher and asked:

"What do you see now, Thuraya?"

"I see nothing but sky," she said, "the blueness of the sky."

He flew with her until he reached his castle. He was a ghoul and his castle a ghoul's palace, a vast palace empty of any human thing. He led her to the topmost room and locked her in. Thuraya became a prisoner. She spent her days sitting at the window. In the morning she watched the ghoul set out to hunt. All through the day she saw not a soul and heard not a sound. In the evening she watched the ghoul return, carrying a cow across his back, and on his shoulder, a tree. He would roast the cow on the embers of the tree, and when he finished gobbling and gulping his meal he would call:

"O Thuraya, beauty fair!

Let down your long, long hair!"

And Thuraya would let down her long hair for the ghoul to climb up.

So it went day after day until one day, while the ghoul was out hunting, Thuraya looked out her window and saw down below, hiding behind a tree, a young man as beautiful as a slice of the moon. He had heard the ghoul calling. She looked down and he looked up. When their eyes met, Thuraya let down her long hair and the handsome young man climbed up to her. They sat next to each other and she told him all that had happened to her and he told her that he had a horse tethered some distance away. All at once, as she looked through the window, Thuraya cried out in alarm:

"I see a cloud of dust. It means the ghoul is on his way! He will eat us both if he sees you here."

Then Thuraya took a deep breath and blew on the youth. The young man was instantly transformed into a pomegranate, battered and worse for wear, which Thuraya tossed among the rest.

Well, the ghoul arrived and after eating his fill he shouted at the top of his voice:

"O Thuraya, beauty fair!

Let down your long, long hair!"

Thuraya let down her hair and the ghoul came up. As soon as he entered he began to sniff around.

"You smell of humans, O Thuraya," he said.

"How could a human find his way here?" she asked. "The smell of humans is in your pockets and on your coat."

The ghoul went on sniffing here and there and said:

"Give me a pomegranate – give me that withered one!"

Thuraya gave him the pomegranate that he pointed to, but when he cut it open she secretly took and kept one seed without his noticing. She transformed her visitor into that one seed and hid it under her pillow.

The next day, Thuraya waited for the ghoul to leave, then she changed the youth back to his human shape. She spent the whole day with him. The time flew by. She screamed when, through the window, she saw the ghoul approaching:

"I see the dust he is kicking up! The ghoul is on his way! I'll transform you into a piece of burnt bread."

She did this and stuck the burnt piece with the rest of the bread.

The ghoul called out:

"O Thuraya, beauty fair!

Let down your long, long hair!"

She let down her long hair and the ghoul climbed up. As he came in he sniffed around and said:

"You smell of humans, O Thuraya!"

"How could a human find his way here?" asked Thuraya, "The smell is on your cloak and in your pockets."

He continued sniffing here and there, and then he said:

"Give me some bread. Give me the burnt piece."

He pointed to the piece he wanted. She gave it to him but kept a bit of crust, into which she transformed the young man. This too she hid under her pillow.

The next morning, Thuraya changed the young man into his human shape again and passed the day with him until the ghoul's return. Once more she was taken by surprise and cried,

"The ghoul is on his way! I see the dust he is kicking up! Let me change you into a pearly pin."

She changed him into a hairpin and stuck it in her hair. The ghoul returned and called:

"O Thuraya, beauty fair!

Let down your long, long hair!"

Thuraya let down her long hair and the ghoul climbed up. He entered sniffing her and said:

"You smell of humans, O Thuraya."

She replied:

"How could a human find his way here?

You chomp all humans till they are dead,

O, for a sword to chop off your head!"

He sniffed and smelled her all over then he said:

"Give me that pin to pick my teeth."

She gave him the pin but kept one pearl. She transformed the youth into the single pearl and hid it under her pillow.

The following morning the ghoul went off and Thuraya returned the young man to his human shape. She said:

"We must leave this place today and flee!"

To make sure that nothing could betray them, Thuraya stained with henna every object in the ghoul's palace. She rubbed henna on pestle and mortar, pitcher and jar, towel and basin, threshold and door latch. But she forgot the broom behind the door. Then she took her comb, her kohl holder, and her mirror and fled with the youth, riding behind him on his horse.

In the evening, the ghoul returned from the hunt as usual, carrying a cow on his back and on his shoulder a tree. He roasted the cow on the embers of the tree; he ate and drank, gobbling and gulping, until he felt full, then he called:

"O Thuraya, beauty fair!

Let down your long, long hair."

The basin responded:

"She is taking a bath!" it said, "She is bathing!"

He called again and the towel said:

"She is drying herself. She is rubbing herself dry!"

The ghoul went on calling and shouting until no object in the place was left to answer him but the broom behind the door:

"Your broom brims with news: the human took her and left!"

The ghoul was enraged. He raced after the pair, running as fast as he could, breaking his toe caps as he ran. Thuraya saw his dust in the distance. The ghoul was catching up. She quickly threw her comb behind her. The comb became a forest thick with trees. But the ghoul gnawed his way through, snapping and chewing one tree after the other until not one sapling was left. On he sped after them. Thuraya threw the kohl vial behind her. It roared into a raging fire. But the ghoul put out the flames, pissing here and pissing there until not one spark was left. On he chased after them. Thuraya threw the mirror behind her. It turned into a lake. The ghoul drowned in the water and died.

So Thuraya and the handsome young man returned to the ghoul's palace and there they lived, a happy pair.

In peace and fruitfulness, many were their joys,
And many were their children, both girls and boys.

WHEN QUEEN MOTHER DIED

We will speak: we have stories to tell,
May our listeners live long and live well.

THERE ONCE WAS A KING – though God alone is Sovereign. This king lived with his aging mother in a great palace in the center of the town. One day the king's mother fell ill, very ill. She sensed that she was about to die. The king was alarmed. Fearing for his mother's life, he summoned the leading physician in the kingdom to treat her. When the doctor came and examined the patient, he said:

"O King of Our Time, your mother's days are numbered. The only remedy we have is to 'change her doorstep' – to take her to some other house. Maybe the Angel of Death will lose track of her and she can be saved."

The king withdrew and sat apart, mournful and distraught. When his vizier saw him in this condition, he inquired what ailed him. The king recounted his trouble and the vizier said:

"O King of the Age, we have to carry out the doctor's prescription!"

"But where shall I send my mother?" asked the king.

"O King of the Age, what a question!" said the vizier. "I will take her into my own mansion and I will not permit the Angel of Death to touch her!"

"My dear vizier," said the king. "I refuse to let my mother die. You may take her. But listen and be warned: you must not bring me news of her death. If you do, I will cut off your head." The vizier moved the king's mother to his house and that same evening she died.

Next morning the vizier was in a quandary; he didn't know what to do. He went out and wandered aimlessly through the streets, trying to think how to break the news to the king that his mother had died; how to do this without having his head cut off. Walking around, he came across a young beggar who looked as bright as the moon at night. The vizier addressed him:

"Young man, will you accept a gold lira to go and tell the king the news about his mother?"

The youth agreed. He pocketed the gold coin and went on his way. Then he began to think to himself:

"They gave me a whole lira of gold for a simple errand like this! There must be some trick or danger involved in the matter."

He went to the souk and bought a shroud which he carried under his cloak. He entered the king's presence saying:

"Peace be with you, O King of the Age!"

The king received him and the young beggar continued:

"O bountiful King,
You own a lamp that is in the vizier's house

A breath of air blew in and now its light is out."

Hearing this, the king wailed at the top of his voice: "My mother has died! My mother is dead!"

Then the beggar said:

"I am a man of honor
My shroud is under my arm
Thank God, that you spoke the words of horror
And that my tongue saved me from harm."

Then the youth pulled the shroud from inside his cloak to demonstrate that he had come prepared to die. The king's anger drained from his heart. All he felt was surprise that a beggar off the street was able to convey news of the death, while his own vizier was at a loss for words and did not know how to tell him that his mother had died. So the king appointed the young beggar to take the vizier's place.

> *Now we have told you all there is to tell*
> *God grant you long lives and mercy on your dead as well.*

THE NIGHTINGALE THAT SPEAKS

LONG AGO, IN A FORMER AGE and a bygone time, there was a king who wished to test the loyalty of his people. He issued a command that for one night no light must show in any part of the city. As no one dared to disobey the royal order, the whole city was plunged into darkness.

On the edge of the town there was a modest house in which three sisters lived by themselves. They earned their living spinning wool. On the night of the king's order, they covered their lamp with a large copper bowl in which they had pierced three holes. Each of the sisters sat by one of the openings, and in this way, they were able to see and continue spinning their wool.

At the palace the king said to his vizier:

"Let us go down to the vault where clothing is stored and dress ourselves like dervishes. Let's see if anyone is breaking our rule."

Wearing clothes in which no one would recognize them, the two men wandered through the city. The only light they saw was a small spark at the edge of the town. Going up to the window of the house, the king and his minister looked inside and saw the young women spinning wool by the dim light of the covered lamp. They listened to them talking to each other.

The oldest was saying:

"If only I could marry the king's baker, then I would eat the finest bread in the land!"

The middle sister said:

"If only I could marry the king's cook, then I would eat the finest food in the land!"

But the youngest sister said:

"For myself, I would not accept anyone as a husband, not even the king's son, unless he agreed to carry my clothes for me on my way to the Turkish bath. Only then would I marry him. And I would bear him a son with one lock of silver in his hair and a daughter with one lock of gold."

Then the girls fell silent and went on with their work by the light from the holes in the copper bowl.

The king told his vizier to note who these sisters were and the next morning he sent a messenger to bring them. When the man summoned the three young women, they went with him, feeling very frightened. On reaching the palace, they found themselves face-to-face with the king and his vizier.

"Peace be with our Sovereign," they said in unison.

The king greeted them and told them that he wanted to make their wishes come true. He asked the oldest sister what she wished for.

"If only I could marry the king's baker," she said, "then I would be eating the finest bread in the land."

The king called the royal baker and said:

"Your wish is granted: here is the king's baker!"

Then he asked the middle sister what her wish was and she said:

"If only I could marry the king's cook, then I would be eating the finest food in the land."

The king called the royal cook and said:

"Your wish is granted: here is the king's cook!"

When he asked the youngest sister the same question, she said:

"For myself, I would not accept anyone as a husband, not even the king's son, unless he agreed to carry my clothes for me on my way to the Turkish bath. Only then would I marry him. And I would bear him a son with a lock of silver in his hair and a daughter with a lock of gold."

The king told the prince:

"Here is your bride!"

"Let us set the date for the wedding," said the king's son, and he carried the youngest sister's clothes to the Turkish bath for her.

All three young women were married on the same day: the eldest to the royal baker, the middle sister to the royal cook, and the youngest to the king's son. There followed days of festivity and nights of celebration and for the duration, no one ate or drank except from the king's kitchen.

It was a happy life until war broke out. The prince was duty-bound to lead his soldiers and defend his country. Before he departed he urged his mother to look after his wife, who was pregnant.

The days passed, one like the other, and the eldest sister grew tired of eating fresh bread and baked goods that were finer than any others. The middle sister, too, was bored by the exceptional food that had no equal and of which there was plenty every day. Envy began to seep into the hearts of the two women, and they started to resent their youngest sister.

The months went by quickly, though as they say, "sooner count the eggs you break into a pan than count the months of a woman's pregnancy." When the day came, the youngest sister gave birth to twins: a boy with a lock of silver in his hair and a girl with a lock of gold.

The jealous sisters arranged with the midwife to substitute a kitten and a puppy for the two infants. The woman took the twins and tucked them into a large wicker basket, which she threw into the river. By the side of the young mother, she placed a kitten and a puppy.

The courier who reached the prince brought him news that his wife had given birth to a kitten and a puppy dog. The prince refused to believe what he heard and he returned home immediately. When he arrived he found his wife in tears and the two little cubs by her side. His heart would not permit him to kill her, so he had her removed to the palace of isolation.

As for the wicker basket, the river swept it up and the current carried it along until it touched shore near a planted garden. The gardener was taken aback to find a basket which had inside it two little infants of radiant beauty. He picked them up and ran to his wife, saying:

"Be happy with the news I bring! God has sent us two children. They will be our family in the years that are left to us."

The gardener's wife kissed them and held them tenderly in her arms. The old couple took care of the children and raised them lovingly. Surrounded with affection and indulgence, the twins flourished: the boy with the lock of silver in his hair and his sister with the lock of gold. They learned to read and write; they also practiced fencing and horseback riding. Time passed and the gardener's wife died and was mourned. When the gardener too was on his deathbed, he called the children to him and explained how he had found them in a wicker basket floating down the river. He showed them where he kept the money he had saved for them to live on and after urging them never to be parted from each other, he kissed them both and died.

The twins continued to live together in the same house. Then one day one of their aunts, their mother's sister, happened to see them as they were walking outside. She followed them to find out where they lived and raced to tell the other aunt what she had discovered:

"I saw them with my own eyes! Twins! With a lock of silver and a lock of gold! They are alive!"

"What if the king finds out?" cried her sister. "He will surely cut off our heads. What can we do?"

They went to the old midwife, asking her to help them in their difficulty. Meeting in secret with the two sisters, the old woman devised a scheme. She made her way to the gardener's house and knocked at the door. The girl was alone. When she opened the door the old woman said:

"My dear, do you have a corner in your house where I can pray? I don't want to miss the midday prayers."

"Please come in, Granny," said the girl, "I bid you welcome!"

When the old woman had done praying she said:

"What a beautiful house you have, God bless it! How well built and spacious!"

The girl was pleased to hear this, so she showed the old woman round; she took her into the bedrooms and to the garden behind the house. Everywhere the old midwife went she was filled with wonder. Each time she admired a part of the house that impressed her she repeated, "It is God's will! Mashallah! It is God's will!" People say this to avert bad luck. She went on:

"My dear child, you possess everything, you lack nothing! The only thing you need for your happiness to be complete is Bulbul as-Siah, the Nightingale that Speaks."

"A nightingale that speaks?" asked the girl in surprise, "Where can I get it?"

"What a question!" said the old woman, "Ask your brother for it! You told me he was the world's best horseman. Let your brother bring it for you!"

And off she went.

Sitting alone in the house, the girl kept thinking about Bulbul as-Siah and crying. She waited impatiently for her brother to come home. When he returned in the evening and asked why she wept, she told him about the strange bird that would make her happiness complete:

"Bring me Bulbul as-Siah, dear Brother," she said, "and I will never ask for anything again!"

"It must live in some faraway place," said her brother, "How can I go and leave you by yourself?"

This made her cry the harder but she went on begging until at last he said:

"Prepare the supplies and get the provisions
For you I'll go to the farthest of regions."

The next morning he packed and set out alone, to faraway countries, beyond his own.

He traversed mountains and valleys and rode across level plains until he came to a parting of the ways. There in the middle of the path sat a ghoul, his hair so long it covered his eyes and his face. The young man saluted the ghoul and said:

"Peace be with you, Uncle Ghoul."

The ghoul said:

"Had not your greeting
Come first before your speaking,
Your flesh and bones I'd now be eating."

The youth approached the ghoul, cleaned his face, cut his hair and altogether sweetened his mood.

"Wonderful! I can see the world again!" said the ghoul.

The young man told his story and explained that he was seeking Bulbul as-Siah.

The ghoul advised him:

"Take this road until you reach an orchard in the grounds of a castle. You will see two birdcages, one made of gold and one of woven cane. Take the cage of cane and don't think of touching the cage of gold."

The youth rode on and on till he came to the orchard. Fruits of every kind and shape hung from the branches of the trees and there before him were the two cages, a bird in each. He said to himself:

"Does it make sense to take the cage of cane and leave the one of gold?"

As soon as he reached with his arm to seize the golden cage, the bird inside awoke and gave a warning shriek. In an instant, the guards protecting the orchard fell upon the boy. They arrested him and took him to the king. The king asked,

"What brought you to this place, young man?"

He answered,

"Believe me, O King of the Age, my motive is not greed but love. I am here for my sister's sake."

He told his story and the king said,

"Good! I will give you Bulbul as-Siah if you bring me the Rice-Bearing Tree."

The young man mounted his horse and left. He crossed hills and valleys until he found himself face-to-face with a ghoul sitting in the middle of the road with one leg pointing to the east and one leg to the west. He saluted the ghoul and the ghoul said:

"Had not your greeting
Preceded your speaking,
The mountaintops and heath
Would hear me crunch your bones between my teeth."

The youth went up to the ghoul and bathed him and cleaned him and offered him a piece of cheese to soften his throat. The ghoul was pleased. When the young man told his story and explained that he was looking for the Rice-Bearing Tree, the ghoul said:

"Continue on this road until you come to a garden alongside a river. There you will find the Rice-Bearing Tree. Break off one small twig and do not think of uprooting the whole tree."

The young man rode and went on riding until he reached the garden. Greenery and grass covered the ground and in the midst of it, white and translucent, stood the Rice-Bearing Tree. Instead of breaking off a small twig, the youth thought:

"Does it make sense to take a twig and leave the tree?"

But the moment he raised his hand to touch it, the tree shuddered and began to rustle. Immediately he was surrounded by guards who seized him and took him to the king. The king asked:

"What brought you to this place, young man?"

He said:

"Believe me, O King of our Time, my reason for coming is not greed but love. I am here for my sister's sake."

He told his story and how he wanted the Rice-Bearing Tree in order to get Bulbul as-Siah, the Nightingale that Speaks. The king said:

"Good! I'll give you the tree if you bring me the daughter of the king of the Far City."

The young man leapt onto his horse and went on his way. When he reached the city gate, he saw an old man sitting by the side of the road, leaning on a cane. The man asked:

"Where are you going, my son?"

The young man answered:

"I am looking for the king's daughter."

"That is a difficult and dangerous quest," said the old man.

The young man said:

"Let me tell you, Uncle, that my motive is not greed but love of my sister. For her sake I am willing to undertake any difficult and dangerous task."

And he explained how he wanted to find the king's daughter in order to get the Rice-Bearing Tree and that he needed the tree to get Bulbul as-Siah. The old man said:

"I can help you but listen to me carefully, my Son! I will be transforming myself into a bird and I will fly with you to the king's daughter. You will enter her room. She will be in front of the mirror combing her hair. If you pluck one hair she will come with you. But do not on any account take more than a single hair!"

The old man stood up and struck the ground with his cane. There was a flash of light so bright that the boy was forced to close his eyes. When he opened them again he saw a large bird spreading its wings and inviting him to mount. He climbed onto the bird's back and was carried through the air until he reached the window of the king's daughter. He alighted carefully and softly entered the room. The king's beautiful daughter was in front of the mirror combing her long black hair. The youth plucked one hair only. The young woman stopped what she was doing but smiled at him in the mirror. The young man froze, overcome by her beauty, unable to breathe. When he took her hand, she came willingly as if she had been expecting him. She rode beside him on the bird's back and so they flew until they reached the king who owned the Rice-Bearing Tree.

The princess stopped at the garden's edge, watching the bird turn into an old man and the old man strike the ground with his cane and turn into a young woman with long black hair exactly like herself.

The youth presented this second girl to the king and in exchange he received a twig off the Rice-Bearing Tree. However, when the king went up to the girl to hold her, she became an old man tapping the ground with his stick. The king was dumbfounded. Then the old man turned into a bird. The princess and the youth rode on his back with the twig off the Rice-Bearing Tree and traveled through the air until they came to the king who owned Bulbul as-Siah. The young woman dismounted and remained in the orchard holding the twig of the Rice-Bearing Tree while the bird changed into a Rice-Bearing Tree. The young man went into the king's presence carrying what the king thought was the Rice-Bearing Tree and he took the cage of woven cane that held Bulbul as-Siah.

When the king went to touch the tree, it became an old man holding a cane to guide him. The king could not believe what he was seeing. The old man changed into a bird once more and carried the princess and the youth on his back with the twig of the Rice-Bearing Tree and the cage of Bulbul as-Siah. They flew a long way above valleys and plains until they reached the boy's sister in the gardener's house. There the bird changed back into his old self again. Brother and sister thanked the old man and bid him goodbye and he returned to his own city.

The sister was overjoyed to see her brother. She kissed him and kissed the princess too. Then she took the twig of the Rice-Bearing Tree and planted it in the garden in front of the house. In the blink of an eye it grew into a large and shady tree with branches stretching to the sky! Next the girl opened the cage of woven cane. Bulbul as-Siah flew out beating his wings and warbling as he fluttered above their heads. He perched on the Rice-Bearing Tree, shaking the grains of rice that sparkled in the sunlight and flashed rainbow colors as they danced to his song.

"Are you perfectly happy now, dear Sister?" asked the young man.

"My happiness will be complete with your happiness when you marry the princess," she replied.

So the young man married the princess, his sister was delighted, and all three were contented living together. The people of the city shared their joy; they came in crowds to witness the wonders of Bubul as-Siah and the Rice-Bearing Tree as well as the radiance of the twin brother and sister with their gold and silver hair.

The news eventually reached the palace. So the king's son decided to go and see for himself. When he arrived he was dazzled by the magical scene: liveliness and color and beauty and happy faces. Suddenly the Nightingale-that-Speaks perched on the Rice-Bearing-Tree right in front of the prince, and looking directly at him, sang:

"I am Bulbul as-Siah.
I bring you no distress
Misfortunes even less
But I ask you to guess:
Is it a likely thing
That the wife of a king
Into the world would bring
A kitten and a puppy dog?
No! She gave birth to a boy and a girl,
One with a lock of silver and one with a golden curl!"

The people stared at the king's son while he looked back at the crowd. Among the rest, his eye fell on a young man with a lock of silver in his hair and next to him a young girl with a lock of gold. The sight troubled and confused him so he ordered the bird:

"Repeat your song, Bird! Sing again!"

The bird raised his head and flapped his wings and repeated in a melodious voice:

"I am Bulbul as-Siah
I bring you no distress
Misfortunes even less

But I ask you to guess:
Is it a likely thing
That the wife of a king
Into the world would bring
A kitten and a puppy dog?
No! She gave birth to a boy and a girl,
One with a lock of silver, one with a golden curl."

The bird then fluttered down to where the twins were standing. At last the king's son understood that these were his own two children, that he had been at fault and had wronged his wife. He ran to his son and daughter and clasped them to his heart and wept. Then they all proceeded to the palace of isolation. The king's son went to his wife and kissed her and asked her forgiveness. He promised that they would live happily to the end of their days with their children beside them.

When the wicked old midwife and the two sisters heard what happened, they exploded in anger and died on the spot.

May you, O listeners, live long and happy lives!

THE DAY IT RAINED DUMPLINGS

It happened or maybe no.
If it did, it was long ago
If not, it could still be so.

THERE WAS A MAN AND HIS WIFE. They were poor and lived in a modest house that was falling into disrepair. But they owned a cow and from her milk they made a modest living. They drank the milk, churned it into butter, made cheese and yoghurt, and any that was left they sold in the souk.

The cow grew old and weak and her milk dried up. So the man and his wife decided to sell her. The man tied a rope round the cow's neck and set off for the cattle market.

He walked along the road pulling the cow behind him. A short distance before reaching the town, he felt tired and decided to take a rest. So he sat down in the shade of a carob tree. Perched in that tree was Umm Suleyman, the owl. She began to hoot:

"Whoo! Whoo!"

"A good morning to you too, Umm Suleyman," the man greeted her in reply.

"Whoo! Whoo!" the owl hooted again.

"The fact is," said the man, "I want to sell this cow for five gold liras."

"Whoo! Whoo!" hooted the owl.

"No need to worry, Umm Suleyman," said the man. "If you don't have the money with you today, I'll come for it tomorrow."

The owl leaned its head to one side and the man said,

"Do you want me to tie the cow here to the tree?"

He looped the cow's lead rope round the trunk of the carob tree and went home to his wife who was anxiously waiting for his news.

"Did you have any luck?" she asked. "Have you sold the cow? How much did you get for her? Who bought her? Tell me!"

"Umm Suleyman bought her," said the man. "She will pay me tomorrow: five gold liras!"

"Only five liras!" exclaimed his wife. "Who is this Umm Suleyman, where does she live?"

"My dear woman, what kind of question is that?" said the man, "Surely you know Umm Suleyman! She is the owl that is perched in the carob tree not far from the entrance to the town."

His wife struck one hand against the other and sighed:

"Why look for sense in a madhouse!"

She dashed out the door and ran without stopping until she heard the owl hooting.

"So this is Umm Suleyman!"

She went on running until she reached the carob tree and saw the cow.

"That is our cow!" she yelled and sprang towards her. But she tripped on what looked like a stone sticking out of the ground.

"This is not a stone!" she exclaimed picking herself up. At her feet she saw a clay pot. She looked inside and she was stunned: it was filled with gold!

"It's a pot of gold!" she whispered, looking right and left. Not a soul in sight! So she picked up the little clay jar, loosened the cow's rope from the tree trunk and headed home laughing to herself all the way.

Once she was inside her house, she locked the door and began to count the gold coins that chance had thrown her way. She could not believe her eyes! When her husband saw what she was doing, he was angered, accusing her loudly:

"You have stolen Umm Suleyman's money! You have stolen Umm Suleyman's money!"

Then he looked outside and saw the cow. He began to shout louder and louder with objections and threats:

"She has stolen the cow as well! I must return them to Umm Suleyman! I must return the cow and the money!"

The man went to get the gold but his wife had hidden it where he could not find it. He told her:

"Tomorrow morning I'll go before the judge and report you!"

What did his wife do? She hurried to the butcher for some meat, and hurried back. Quickly she mixed the meat with onions and cracked wheat to make kibbeh dough. Quickly she shaped the dough into balls the size of dumplings, fried them and scattered them on the ground in front of the house. When she had done that, she called to her husband who was working in their little plot of meadow in the back:

"Come, dear husband! Come and take a look! It has been raining kibbeh!"

The man came round, picked up a dumpling and took a bite.

"This is excellent kibbeh, by God." He said. "It has been an age since I tasted meat."

"May it bring you good health, dear husband," said the wife. "I wish you the best of health!"

And so the man ate one ball of kibbeh after another enjoying himself and commenting:

"How delicious this is! And it is still warm! Imagine, raining kibbeh and it is still warm!"

His wife urged him to eat more:

"Eat your fill! The best of health to you!"

He ate until he was sated and went to bed a happy man.

But next day he resumed his accusations, telling his wife:

"You have stolen Umm Suleyman's money! Stolen property

must be returned to its rightful owners! I am going to report you to the judge!"

To this she made no reply. The man went before the judge and listed his grievances. So they sent for his wife to verify the accusations. They asked:

"Where did you hide Umm Suleyman's money?"

"Umm Suleyman?" she asked. "Who is this Umm Suleyman? And what money are you talking about?"

The man was furious. He said that his wife was lying:

"She is a liar and a hypocrite! She is a cheat and a swindler!"

They began to argue in front of the judge then the wife said quietly:

"Please, Your Honor, ask him when this theft took place."

So the judge asked:

"When was the money stolen?"

"It was on the day it rained dumplings, it rained kibbeh," said the man.

"What was that?" said the judge, "Did you say on the day it rained kibbeh?"

"Yes," repeated the man. "And the kibbeh was still warm!"

The judge thought how strange it is that men should be so simple compared with women and their many wiles. He dismissed the husband from his court. The man was disappointed but went home with his wife. To cheer him up the woman said:

"Let us both go to town tomorrow and together sell the cow. And let us call on Umm Suleyman on the way. What do you say?"

This reassured him and he went to bed happy and at peace – not only he, but his wife also.

There I left them and came very fast
To tell you their story from first to last.